MW01128876

1

The Rock & Roll Chronicles

A Novel

© 2012

David Malcolm Rose

davidmalcolmrose(at)yahoo(dot)com

"Rock & Roll fosters totally negative and destructive reactions in young people. It is written, played and sung, for the most part, by cretinous goons."

Frank Sinatra, 1957

"I don't care what people say.
Rock & Roll is here to stay."

Danny and the Juniors, 1958

4

Chapter 1

October 1958

It was cold, much colder than one would expect for an October morning. Officer Bolachko hunched his shoulders and settled once again against the door. The car was poorly made, and the wind drove icy daggers through the cracks.

"I would not put too much faith in that door latch," Sergeant Kostonka said without taking his eyes off the street.

Bolachko straightened in the seat, "If you don't mind me asking, Comrade Kostonka, why are we parked here in this particular spot, and just what is it we are watching for?"
It was a legitimate question. Kostonka had circled the block twice while waiting for a delivery truck to clear what appeared to be an unremarkable parking place on Kulakov Street. Twice around a block of nearly identical soot-stained, gray concrete apartment buildings with dozens of nearly identical empty parking places along each leg of the journey.

"We watch for what doesn't belong," Kostonka replied.

Bolachko let out a heavy sigh and regretted the action almost immediately. His moist breath froze white on the inside of the windshield. It was happening right in front of his eyes, and he watched the hoary crystals form. They looked bright white against the slate-colored background of empty street, lifeless buildings, and overcast October sky. As he watched, the white crystals intensified and then flickered golden yellow, so brilliant he had to blink and look away. Bolachko shifted his gaze across the street and upward.

As was typical for this part of the city, the four-story, unadorned apartment buildings formed a palisade of cold concrete. A palisade that was almost unbroken but not quite. He hadn't noticed it before but there was a vacant lot in the place where the third unit in from the corner had once stood. It was like a missing tooth in a dirty gray smile. Bolachko could see the silhouettes of the by-gone apartments still etched on the wall of the intact building to the south of the gap. They were the same floor plan as many Muscovite apartments, the same as his own.

In the back were the remains of a column of kitchens, top to bottom. The outlines of long-gone stoves were visible, stenciled in grease on the green walls. Up the center of the surviving building, the outline of a stairwell could be seen. The missing steps were clearly delineated in flaking green paint. On each of the ghost stairwell landings, the grimy pistachio walls were highlighted by squares of somewhat cleaner paint. There was one square on each floor.

Bolachko knew the clean squares marked the spots where framed posters of happy peasants working for the revolution once hung. If asked to do so he could name the prints that hung on each landing of the stairwell; first floor, *Wheat Harvest in Ukraine*; second floor, *Tractor Factory*; third floor, *Women Defense Workers*; fourth floor, *Lenin Speaks to the People*.

The most striking thing about the view was not the vacant lot or the ghostly outlines of the lost building; the most striking thing was the sun. Just above the eastern horizon, the gunmetal blanket of clouds was breaking up allowing the sun to come through the gap in the wall of dingy apartments. The sunlight melted the frost from the windscreen and filled the interior of the small car. Bolachko could feel the warmth almost immediately.

"We park here for the sun," Kostonka said.
The shaft of sunlight, only slightly wider than the black police car, intensified as the clouds broke away. The sun rose and bathed the squad car with warmth. The raw wind diminished somewhat. It wasn't long before both men loosened their scarves and unbuttoned their coats.

Kostonka rolled the window down a few inches on his side of the car and lit a harsh, Bulgarian cigarette. Bolachko looked down at the naked spline where the handle for the window on his side should have been. Without being asked, Kostonka pulled the driver-side window handle loose and passed it over to his new partner. The younger officer accepted the handle and rolled down the window on his side as well. The cross draft

7

chilled the car and drew the cigarette smoke toward the passenger compartment. Bolachko rolled up his window and returned the handle.

At the end of the block, Rurrik Zimas turned the corner onto Kulakov Street. His posture changed almost immediately as the sun hit him and he felt its warmth. His shoulders relaxed and the hand that held his thin coat tightly around his thin neck loosened its grip. Rurrik stopped, closed his eyes, and lifted his face to the sun. The inside of his eyelid glowed orange and he could feel the sun's power spreading through his body. He rocked back and forth on his heels as if to pump the warmth and energy to the farthest reaches.

The first thing he saw upon opening his eyes was the black car. His chill returned. The sun's glare on the windows prevented him from seeing the occupants but the smoke curling from the window told him the vehicle was not empty. Experience told him this dark sedan was something to be avoided. The young Russian once again pulled his coat tightly around his body, quickly crossed the street, and hurried down the sidewalk on the shaded side.

Back in the black sedan Officer Kostonka caught his partner's attention. "When given a choice, on a morning like this, what man chooses the shade over the sunlight?" he mused.

Rurrik walked rapidly, his face turned away from the black car. At a building near the end of the second block, he stopped, looked back briefly, climbed the steps, and worked his key in the poorly made lock. Inside, on the first floor, he passed the poster of *Wheat Harvest in Ukraine* and doffed his cap to the stout farmers and their solid-looking wives. Rurrik took the stairs two at a time. He turned on the second landing and flexed his thin biceps to mimic the burly men in the *Tractor Factory*. On the third floor, he stopped briefly to blow a kiss to the poster of *Women Defense Workers*.

At the top of the stairs, just across from *Lenin Speaks to the People*, he slowed his pace and readied his apartment key. Rurrik hunched his back as if to hide what he was doing from the steely eyes of Lenin. The key was just a prop. There were no locks on his door, at least none that worked. He owned nothing worthy of such security.

His room was somewhat warmer than the street had been and almost as austere. A single cot with rusting iron frame, a wooden nightstand, a chair, and a small table made up the bulk of the decor. All featured the same flat green paint as the walls. A dresser, with three of the four original drawers still in attendance, completed the furnishings. There was an ornate mirror above the dresser, but the frame was battered and most of the silver was gone from the top half of the glass. A small closet, its door missing one of the hinge pins, jutted from a corner. A metal-framed window facing the street and a door leading down a short hall to the kitchen were the apartment's only other amenities.

The most unusual thing about the room, other than its bleakness, was the walls. They were, everywhere, dappled with short pieces of stiff masking tape. Some of the segments of tape still held the corners of photographs on cheap, magazine paper. Complementing the masking tape dapple was an equal sprinkling of shallow craters where pieces of tape had been pulled off completely. In places, the tape had peeled the flawed paint from the wall right on down to the masonry. The only variation in the pattern was on the long wall next to the bed. Here, secured with new masking tape, were half a dozen photos cut neatly from American Rock & Roll magazines. Jerry Lee Lewis, Little Richard, and Elvis smiled, sang, and gyrated from their assigned posts on the apartment wall.

Rurrik took a package from beneath his coat and placed it on the bed. Next, he removed his wool cap, pulled a nylon comb from his back pocket, and looking in the remains of the mirror, combed the dark hair on the sides of his head back into duck tails. Next, he combed the hair on top of his head forward and twisted it into a hairworm over his forehead.

Rurrik pulled the frayed string which hung from the ceiling fixture turning on the single bulb. Walking over to the window, he lowered the tattered shade. Only then, in the artificial twilight, did he feel safe in opening the package on the bed. The slick, black vinyl record with the crisp checkerboard pattern on the label stood in sharp contrast to the dingy copy of Pravda which had concealed it. Rurrik cleared the last of the paper wrapping and placed the record gently back down onto the bed.

The closet door with its missing hinge pin was tricky to use, but Rurrik liked it that way. He opened the door by holding it upright and walking it slowly outward. Stepping inside the closet, he turned back toward the room and lifted a box down from a shelf above the door. It was a child's windup record player fitted in its own cardboard suitcase. The machine was well worn but serviceable.

The biggest problem would be that the player ran 78 RPM while the record with the checkered label was a 45. Rurrik placed the record player on the floor, wound it as tightly as prudence would allow, and put the record on. He turned the volume up and started the record on the outermost groove. The cheap speaker hissed as the record rumbled and popped. The pop was caused by a scratch on the record and Rurrik used it to judge the speed of the turntable. Pop..pop..pop..pop - 78 RPM. He quickly lifted the needle from the vinyl before the actual recording started.

Rurrik ripped a corner from the discarded newspaper and folded it into a small wedge. He slid the wedge across the deck of the machine and part of the way into the space below the turntable. The young man started the record again. Pop.... pop.... pop.... pop. The friction from the wedge had slowed the turntable. About 60 RPM Rurrik judged. Lost in concentration, he almost forgot to lift the tone arm. He deftly snatched it up just before the actual recording began. Rurrik pushed the wedge in farther to tighten the fit and increase the friction. He restarted the record. Pop......pop......pop......pop, close enough.

Rurrik pulled up the arm, rewound the record player, and started the 45 again. He turned the volume down to one of its lower settings and leaned in toward the small speaker. The hypnotic rhythm of the baseline started and then the hambone guitar came in sounding sharp clear chords; Bomp-Ba-Ba-Babom Bomp-Bomp. While still on his hands and knees, Rurrik began to tap his fingers on the sides of the little machine.

An earthy voice transcended the paper speaker. *"Everything's gonna be alright."*
The young Russian began to nod his head and roll his shoulders in time to the music; Bomp-Ba-Ba-Babom Bomp Bomp. He reached over and turned the volume up a notch.

"If I can just make it till Friday night."
Rurrik came up onto his knees, arched his back, and strummed the strings of an imaginary guitar.

Bomp-Ba-Ba-Babom Bomp Bomp.

He leaned forward to turn the volume up just one more notch but, caught up in the music, turned it up two instead.

Rurrik, as if lifted by the song, sprang to his feet and threw his coat off and across the bedstead. He swung the imaginary guitar over his head and back down as he struck the make-believe strings in time with the record.

"*Whistle blows and I get my pay*," the cheap speaker crackled.

Rurrik spread his legs and moved backward in a series of quick, short hops holding his invisible guitar out in front of him like a rifle and bayonet.

"BOMP-BA-BA-BABOM BOMP BOMP."

Rurrik took two quick steps forward, went down on his knees, and slid to a stop in front of the record player. He spun the volume dial to the max.

"*I'm a gonna rock my blues away*," the speaker rasped.

Rurrik sprang up from his knees into a squat and began to hop across the room still striking the make-believe guitar that he now held at his side.

BOMP-BA-BA-BABOM BOMP BOMP.

As the record built to a climax he sprang into the air, windmilling the guitar and landing in a split in the middle of the floor.

BOMP-BA-BA-BABOMP BOMP-**BAM**!

The door of the apartment burst open. Sergeant Kostonka and Officer Bolachko stood in the doorway looking down at Rurrik Zimas. Ker-klunk, ker-klunk, ker-klunk; the needle bounced as the record continued to turn oblivious to the fact that the song had ended.

Bolachko walked over and pushed down the lid of the record player with the toe of his heavy-soled, black shoe. The needle ripped painfully across the 45. The younger officer picked up the player and stuck it under his arm. The wind-up motor labored momentarily and then died.

"How have you been, Rurrik?" Kostonka asked as he lit a cigarette and offered one to Rurrik.

Rurrik shifted out of the split into a seated position. He declined the cigarette with a wave of his hand. "I've been well enough, and yourself?"

"Well enough," Kostonka replied, "Have you met my new partner, Officer Bolachko?"

"I don't believe I have had the pleasure."

Bolachko sniffed as if something bad were in the air. He moved over to the dresser and began to pull the drawers out one at a time and turn them upside down on the bed. As he turned up the bottom drawer half a dozen 45 records slid off the pile of clothes and onto the floor. Bolachko picked one up and read the label. "Little Reeshard?"

"Little Richard," Rurrik corrected. "He is a Rock & Roll star from Georgia."

"Georgia, here in the Soviet Union?"

Rurrik winced. "No, Georgia in the USA."

The younger officer dropped the record he was holding and picked up two records that were markedly different than the others. They were cut on a thinner, more flexible vinyl and the hole in the center looked to have been made by a burning cigarette. He held it up to the ceiling light and saw a whitish-gray image on a dark gray background.

"What kind of record are these? It looks like X-ray."

"Those are ribs," Kostonka explained.

"No disrespect, Comrade Kostonka," Bolachko countered. "But this is hip joint, not ribs"

"Yes, of course," the older man replied. "They are records made on X-ray film. Ribs are what such homemade recordings are called. They are also forbidden."

"This I did not know," Rurrik said unconvincingly.

Bolachko dropped the ribs back into the pile and stepped over to the pictures on the wall, grinding the records under his feet as he went. "Do you have a problem with Russian music?" he asked the young refusenik.

Rurrik winced as the records cracked.

"At one time Rurrik had considerable talent in the musical arts," Kostonka explained, "He trained for a while in the Bolshoi."

Bolachko sniffed again and poked his thumb at one of the pictures on the wall. It was a black and white photo of Elvis Presley and Sam Phillips sitting at what looked to be a table in a cafe. They were smiling at the camera. A young Asian-American woman in a waitress uniform was filling their coffee cups from a glass decanter with a black Bakelite handle and a starburst design on the side. Bolachko pointed at Elvis "Is this Little Reeshard?"

Rurrik hung his head. "That is Elvis and Mr. Sam Phillips"

"Is that your girlfriend, the Chinese? How beautiful. Do you kiss her good night when you go to bed?" Bolachko ripped the photo from the wall, balled it up, and dropped it on the bed.

This wasn't Rurrik's first arrest. He knew Kostonka and a few other members of the Moscow City Police. He had not met Bolachko before, but the type was recognizable. Russia produced many young people who were optimistic and took their work seriously. Rurrik looked over at Kostonka with a knowing smile.

"Why don't you get your coat so we can go down to the station?" Kostonka invited. Rurrik snatched his coat from the bedstead, but the lining hung up on the rusty metal newel. The thin fabric ripped, and the garment fell onto the bed. As he retrieved the coat Rurrik deftly scooped up the discarded photo of Elvis as well.

As they left the apartment Bolachko drug his hand along the wall peeling off the remaining Rock & Roll photos as he went.

CHAPTER 2

The cramped cell was as cold as a tomb. There was a small, barred window up high and a concrete bench down low, but other than those two features and the door, the cubicle offered little worthy of comment.

Rurrik sat sideways on the bench with his legs drawn up against the cold. He looked at the wall next to his head. Everywhere in Moscow concrete could be found and almost all of it was bad. There was poorly mixed concrete with the consistency of old cake and more that looked like moldy cheese. There was poorly formed concrete riddled with air holes, some big enough to swallow your fist. There was concrete that was poured when it was too hot or too cold and it flaked off as easily as the cheap paint that inevitably covered it. The part of the city that wasn't cast in substandard concrete was laid up in bricks or stone. The bricks were universally bad and tended to pop off circular chips with the season's first frost. In places, these chips lay on the sidewalk below the wall like autumn leaves. Some of the stone was of quality but the majority of the mortar in the joints was so decrepit that one could scratch it out with a house key and grind it to sand between the fingers. It seemed as if the only masonry work of quality in all of Moscow was this cell. The walls shone like flint behind a skin of brownish green moisture.

Rurrik was grateful to Sergeant Kostonka for allowing him to get his coat when they left the apartment. The cell would have been intolerable without it. Kostonka was not a bad man, he was a survivor and survivors don't make enemies unnecessarily, even if that enemy was someone as lowly as Rurrik Zimas. Officer Bolachko, on the other hand, was quite a different case. He was young, only five or six years older than Rurrik himself, and eager to please his superiors. As a result, he did his job well, too well. "He won't last long," Rurrik thought to himself with some satisfaction.

Bolachko's ambition would soon bring him into a confrontation with the mass of inertia, which makes up the bulk of Moscow's police force, the bulk of the entire Soviet state for that matter. That course stone ground even the choicest grain into the same poor-quality meal. Officer Bolachko would be no exception, but during the time it took for that slow turning wheel to get the better of him, he could be dangerous.

Time for Rurrik no longer existed. About five days, more or less, had passed since he had been placed in the cell. Although it was his first time in this particular cell it was not his first trip to the lower levels of the Prospekt Street sub-station. Down here the act of waiting can drive a man crazy. Rurrik had learned early on that the only way to keep from waiting was to suspend time. He could be here for five more hours, five days, or five years. That he would stay here five years was unlikely. At some point, they would need the cell for a new arrival. In the meantime, there was not a thing he could do about it and when nothing can be done, the wise man does nothing.

Rurrik took the photo of Elvis from the torn lining of his coat, laid it on his knee, and carefully flattened it with his fingers. Elvis Presley was not unknown in Russia. The papers in Moscow had written much about American Rock & Roll and all of it was bad news for the United States and good news for Russia. Rock & Roll was living proof of Western depravity and Elvis was the high priest of this decadent cult. If the papers were to be believed, the music was turning the American youth into animals, and it would not be long before the civilization collapsed as a result. The United States, that great, misguided experiment in democracy, would collapse inward on itself. It would rot out from the inside as a summer squash left too long in the field.

Rurrik did not make a habit of believing the Soviet press, few Russians did. He admired everything about Elvis, the singer was so American. He had come up from next to nothing and made it to the top. We all live in this world, but few men truly walk upon the earth. Elvis did.

Elvis was a hero to Rurrik but right now the cups of hot coffee on the table in the photograph looked inviting. He had heard unflattering things about American coffee, that it was thin and tasteless, but to a man with no coffee at all, it appeared to be rich and dark. Rurrik's gaze shifted from the cups to the coffee pot and then up to the girl in the waitress uniform. He had never seen a young woman so wholesome and yet so exotic. Bolachko was right, she was beautiful. The young prisoner lay down on the bench and studied the photograph.

Outside the small, high, window water could be heard dripping slowly down a metal drainpipe. Above that somewhere was the sound of a toilet running. Rurrik focused on the two sounds, first one and then the other. Each had its own pattern and when they melded a third, a more richly woven pattern emerged. In his mind, he separated the two patterns and then combined them into the third. He did this over and over again, setting up a complex rhythm. To this rhythm he added a back-beat, tapping his foot both heel and toe.

Rurrik was completely immersed in the sounds when another rhythm worked its way into the water music. It was a rhythm that he recognized, the sound of hobnailed boots descending stone steps. He held his breath and listened. There were two distinct sets of boots and they paused as they reached the bottom of the steps. The boots started up again and grew louder as they approached his cell. The young refusenik focused on the door. The boots were right outside now but they weren't stopping, they passed by. Rurrik let out his breath as quietly as possible. It was not, however, a sigh of relief. Being passed over by the boots could be as bad as being selected by them. Beyond the door, the sound of the boots began to fade and then suddenly stopped. Once again Rurrik held his breath. Out in the corridor, few words were spoken and the boots returned.

Rurrik's cell door was thrown open. A soldier in a drab gray-brown uniform stepped in. The prisoner could see a second soldier standing just outside the door. "Rurrik Zimas?" the first soldier asked.

Rurrik nodded in confirmation.

"You will come." The soldier asserted.

CHAPTER 3

Although it was unmarked the Central Headquarters building took up the entire south side of the square on Novokuznetsk
Street. It was not one building but half a dozen separate structures interconnected like a rabbit warren. This sprawling laby-
rinth was known to house certain offices of the Moscow Police,
the Soviet Army's Intelligence branch, and the KGB. At times
it was difficult for the comrade-in-the-street to tell where one
agency left off and the other began. It was not that the three
agencies worked together, they did not, but infiltrators, spies,
and counterspies wove the triad into a tapestry of espionage and
duplicity. Who was really running the show was a puzzling
question but one far too dangerous to be asked.

Kostonka had once again found the perfect parking place,
this one tucked behind a food kiosk across the square from Central Headquarters. From where Bolachko and Kostonka now sat
the main entrance to the building could be seen beyond the
statue of Lenin in the square. The statue and kiosk made it difficult for their black sedan to be seen from the entrance to the
Headquarters. The two officers could watch without being
watched and in Soviet Russia, this was always a distinct advantage.

As a bonus, the food kiosk provided coffee and soup. The coffee was bitter and the soup thin but both were hot. Kostonka ordered a cup of cabbage soup and flashed his badge by way of payment. He returned to the car, removed the course paper napkin from around the cup, blotted some of the congealing grease from the top of the soup, and offered the cup to Bolachko.

"This stuff will keep you regular."
Bolachko glanced briefly at the soup and then focused his gaze back across the square. A brown car with a red star on the door stopped in front of the Central Headquarters Building. The driver, a man in military dress the same color as the car, got out and opened the back door on the passenger's side. A thin young man stumbled down from the car accompanied by a second soldier.

"Is that your friend Zimas?" Bolachko asked.

Kostonka looked up from his cup, a thin oily slick clinging to his lip. "I believe you are right. It is him and he is in the company of the Soviet Army's police. Perhaps Comrade Plotkovic would be interested in this information."

"Do you mean Colonel Plotkovic? Is he not KGB?" Bolachko asked.

"You must learn to view information like currency. We have found a coin in the street and must look to spend it wisely," Kostonka said.

"But what connection could Zimas have with the KGB?" Bolachko asked.

"Perhaps it would be best to hear Comrade Plotkovic's opinion on that."

Kostonka drove around the square, past the Central Headquarters building, and made a right-hand turn at the corner. In the middle of the block, he turned right once again, this time down an alley, and parked in front of a useless loading dock made of crumbling concrete. The two policemen picked their way up through the rubble of the dock and entered the Headquarters by way of a small door.

Kostonka took the lead down corridors, through doorways, and then up a narrow set of stairs. Bolachko was surprised at how quickly the older officer climbed. On the fourth floor, Kostonka eased open a metal door that led to an expansive hallway flanked by large, wooden office doors with windows of frosted glass. As they started down the hallway, they could hear footsteps echoing from the ornate marble steps at the far end. The sound of steps grew louder and Kostonka pulled Bolachko through one of the wooden doors, the one that had Colonel Plotkovic lettered on the frosted glass.

The lettering on the glass was sloppy, the paint uneven. At one time, Mother Russia could produce craftsmen that rivaled any in the world, but little evidence of that was seen anymore. This lettering, however, was more than just indifference. The many who painted Plotkovic's name had clearly despised the man.

The old policeman quickly closed the door behind Bolachko and himself. The room they entered was a small outer office with a connecting door and one wooden desk. The desk was un-occupied and empty except for a brown phone with no rotary dial mechanism.

Kostonka turned, eased the door to the hall slightly open again, and peeked through the crack. Bolachko peered over the smaller man's shoulder. The two soldiers flanking Rurrik reached the top of the stairs and started down the hall. At the first door on the right, the threesome turned and entered. "What office is that?" Bolachko asked.

"I do not know that one. The last time I was here it was empty." Kostonka said.

As they watched, the two soldiers came out through the office door and turned back toward the marble steps. "So, the Soviet Army has an interest in Rurrik Zimas the refusenik. What concern is that to us?" Bolachko said.

"Zimas! Rurrik Zimas is here in this building?" Anton Plot-kovic had entered the small office through the connecting door. His voice took the younger officer by surprise and Bolachko spun quickly around. Kostonka, on the other hand, did not leave his post at the peephole. "Colonel Plotkovic, meet my new partner Officer Bolachko," Kostonka said as he silently shut the office door and turned to face the Colonel.

Plotkovic was no taller than Kostonka but thinner and with a neatly trimmed beard and mustache. He did not acknowledge Bolachko's extended hand but focused on Kostonka instead.

"What is Zimas doing at the Central Headquarters building?"

Kostonka seemed to ignore the question. "I served under Colonel Plotkovic in the Great Patriotic War." He explained to Bolachko and then turned to Plotkovic. "Who is in the office across the hall, the one that was empty, the one near the front stairwell?"

"Belov," Plotkovic said. A twitch developed in the corner of his left eye. "Did Zimas go in there?"

"Our old friend General Belov of Military Intelligence has joined you here on the fourth floor?" Kostonka said. "How very nice for you."

"Yes, he is the new army liaison officer." Plotkovic began to nervously tug at the whiskers on his chin. "I must know what Belov is up to. You two must find this out for me."

"But we are simple officers of the Moscow City Police. This seems to be a matter better addressed by your men here at the KGB," Kostonka said.

"Yes, well, until I am sure of the nature of this matter, I would prefer to keep it confidential. I will have you transferred to my command for temporary duty," Plotkovic picked up the handpiece of the phone on the desk.

"Will this temporary duty include an increase in pay?" Kostonka asked.

***

Inside Belov's office, Rurrik was escorted quickly past the reception area and into the office of the General. The old man looked up from behind the large wooden desk that sat in front of an arch-topped window hung with heavy burgundy drapes. The general was in his late sixties with clipped gray hair and sharp gray eyes. Despite his age, he was still a powerful man and sat upright in the brown leather chair. There were two large wooden chairs in front of the desk but Rurrik was not asked to sit. The General dismissed the soldiers with a slight nod of his head.

"It is good to see you back in Moscow," Rurrik said after the soldiers had gone. Although he had not seen the older man for some time, Rurrik had known General Belov for as long as he could remember. The old man had been Rurrik's father's commanding officer during the war against the Fascists.

"How is your mother, Rurrik?" General Belov asked.

"She is well. As well as can be expected," Rurrik answered. Belov's office was warm, warmer than anyplace Rurrik had been in days. He opened his coat to allow his chilled body to absorb as much of the heat as possible. Belov invited him to sit, and he did.

"I was saddened when I heard about her," the general continued. "She was one of the greatest dancers the Bolshoi has ever known. And so young."

"Yes, the doctors say she was young for such a stroke, but they take very good care of her in the institution."

"Do you visit with her often?" The older man asked.

"Yes, I do. On Wednesday and Sunday when I am off from work. When the weather is nice, I go with her to the park. I think she likes it there," Rurrik shrugged with resignation.

"And you Rurrik, you also had potential in the ballet. We were all surprised when you quit," the old general stated as he looked down at the folder on his desk. "An arrest for driving a taxicab without license or permit and then another arrest for teaching dance also without license or permit. What kind of dance were you teaching?"

"Modern Dance."

"And just what is modern dance?"

"In Russia, it is any dance that is less than two hundred years old."

Now it was the old man's turn to shrug. "In that case, it is much like Russia's modern military strategy." General Belov shifted forward in his leather chair and placed his arms on his desk. "And now we must deal with the problem at hand. I am

31

told that you are here because you were once again arrested with contraband in your possession."

"A few American Rock & Roll records. Hardly enough to threaten the great Union of Soviet Socialist Republics."

Belov leaned back in his chair. "Your father was a good man and a good friend to me. He was also a hero to this country, a real hero in The Great Patriotic War. He had many friends, powerful friends, but a man with powerful friends also has powerful enemies. You were not yet a man when your father died and you don't know of such things, but I must tell you, you are being careless with your freedom, perhaps with your life."

"I have no enemies other than the Moscow Police and they don't seem to have any ambitions beyond stepping on my record collection," Rurrik explained.

"You would not have to look far to find enemies," Belov cautioned. "Just down the hall in this very building is the office of Anton Plotkovic of the KGB."

"I do not know Plotkovic, and I see no reason why he would know of me."

"And yet he does," the general countered. "He was a man bound for military greatness until your father exposed his cowardice. That is a fatal flaw for a man with aspirations to rise in military service. He was forced to leave the army and take a position in the government."

"A coward? In our KGB?" Rurrik said with mock surprise.

"For members of the KGB cowardice is not a handicap, it is almost considered a virtue," Belov said. "But do not take this lightly. Plotkovic is a clever and resourceful man."

"I am sure that he is, but why would he bother with me? I am but a humble servant of the state."

The old general leaned back in his chair and sighed. "And how do you serve the state, in this humble manner?"

"I work at the Kazan railway station. I organize the misplaced baggage and mop out the vannaya in the morning and once again at night."

"That is even more humble than I thought." The general shook his head and, again, looked back down at the file that lay open on his desk. "After the academy, the state sent you to school to become an automobile mechanic. You did well; top of your class, but then you quit that also."

"If you own a Soviet automobile, you do not need a mechanic, you need a priest," Rurrik observed.

"Unfortunately, the state has banned the practice of religion." Belov studied Rurrik for a long minute then looked back to the folder. "So, you know of American Rock & Roll music?"

"Yes, I have had an interest for quite some time."

"And to understand the songs you must learn some English?"

"Yes, I have learned some English from the records and the magazines." Rurrik had no idea why Belov would be asking such things or where this conversation was headed but he knew the general was a person he could trust. Perhaps he was the only person Rurrik could trust.

"The magazines?" Belov asked.

"Rock & Roll magazines."

General Belov once again leaned forward in his chair. "What would you think of joining the glorious Army of the Soviet Union? I could arrange for you to be under my command and once you are under my command Plotkovic cannot reach you. I have an assignment that I believe would interest you. An assignment for a man with your interests and knowledge."

"General Belov, I know you were a friend of my father and that you are acting because of that friendship but I don't think the military would be such a good match for me."

Belov picked up the folder from his desk, opened it, and glanced at the first page. "You are twenty-one years old next month. It is old enough for a man to make his own decisions." He closed the folder and dropped it onto his desk. "You are free to go but, Rurrik, be careful."

The old general came out from behind his desk, took Rurrik by the arm, and walked with him to the door. "Plotkovic is not a man who forgets, and he would think nothing of sending oxen to cultivate a flower box. He is also a man who would enjoy punishing the son for the sins of the father. It was only by chance that I found you this time. If Plotkovic gets you in a cell again I might not find you at all."

At the door, Belov handed Rurrik a card. "Remember to give my best to your mother and if you change your mind about joining the army be sure and give me a call."

Rurrik accepted the card and shook the old man's hand. "I will. I will do both."

CHAPTER 4

Out in the hallway, the soldiers were gone. Rurrik listened to the rhythmic echo of his own footsteps as he started down the concrete stairwell at the end of the corridor. "Hey, Hey, Baby," he sang and smiled at the reverberation. The acoustics were marvelous. "Hey, Hey, Hey, Baaaby," he sang even louder, landing flatfooted and heavy on each step in time with his own song. Feeling his freedom, the young man filled the stairwell with music as he descended.

Two floors down he began to feel a chill and stopped to pull on his worn coat. As Rurrik work his arm carefully through the torn lining of the sleeve he was sure he heard the sound of a door opening in the stairwell above him. The young Russian ceased his motion and listened. It was so quiet he could hear the beating of his heart.

Rurrik hastily donned his coat, pushing the torn lining out the sleeve hole ahead of his hand. He continued down the stairs taking them two at a time. Now he did not sing. He was sure he heard footsteps on the stairs above him. Near the bottom, Rurrik stopped once again and looked up. The footsteps stopped as well. He saw nothing but a coil of concrete steps and balustrade.

As Rurrik crossed the lobby he ripped the torn lining that flapped from the end of his sleeve and threw it in the direction of a refuse container. He did not look back but kept his eyes on the glass doors that led out onto Novokuznet Street. In its reflection, he could watch the stairwell behind him. No one appeared.

Out on the street, the young Russian hurried toward the south. He did not dare to turn around but tried to watch the sidewalk behind by glancing in the rear-view mirrors of parked cars as he passed. He saw nothing. At the corner of Valovaya Street, a number nine Moscow city bus was just pulling to a stop. He climbed aboard and took a seat in the rear. Only when the bus had begun to move did he dare to look back. Two men in heavy, dark coats and hats turned the corner from Novokuznet Street. Rurrik rose up for a better view, but just as he did a plume of blue-black smoke from the exhaust pipe of the bus obscured the view.

Rurrik sat back and tried to relax. Even in the back of the bus, sitting above the engine, it was cold enough for him to see his breath. "Those men had no interest in me. They may have looked like police but everyone in Moscow who has a heavy coat is wearing it today," he told himself. He folded his arms, leaned forward, and took deep breaths to ease the tightness in his chest.

He picked a discarded copy of *Izvestia* from the floor and opened it in order to hide his face. *Izvestia*, which meant "News", was the official newspaper of the Soviet State while *Pravda*, which meant "Truth", was the mouthpiece of the Communist party. It was said in Russia that there was no news to be found in *Izvestia* and no truth to be found in *Pravda*. To most Russians, the papers were interchangeable.

The copy that Rurrik was using for a disguise featured an article about the native peoples of the American west, Indians they were called. It told of how these Indians had been robbed of their land and forced to live in poverty in the most remote portions of the desert. There was a picture accompanying the article.

In the picture was a small house made of mud bricks. Off of one side of the house was a porch with a dirt floor and woven brush for a roof. Beyond the mud brick house stretched a seemingly endless landscape of terraced cliffs, rocky spires, and flat-topped mountains. A woman sat beneath this brush arbor in the picture, and she did, indeed, look poor. She wore a black broad-brimmed hat and her deeply lined face was turned up toward the sun.

Rurrik loved articles like this when they also featured pictures. He let his mind wander out into the sun-drenched landscape and felt the warmth. He did not, however, dream of one day going to America. Such a thing would have been beyond even his most desperate dreams.

The number nine bus went within five blocks of Donskoi Institution where his mother resided. It was not one of his usual days for the Donskoi but his stay with the Moscow police had thrown off his schedule. Rurrik decided to make the best of this impromptu bus trip and go visit. He got off the bus at Gorky Park and walked to the south toward the Institute.

A black sedan with the motor running was parked a block beyond the entrance to the institution. The low sun reflecting from the windshield prevented him from seeing the occupants. Rurrik angled as he crossed the street and tried to disappear into the shadows against the building. At the entrance to the Donskoi, he ducked out of the shadows and quickly climbed the stairs to the front doors.

Inside the Institute the reception desk was deserted. This was unusual and Rurrik found himself in a heightened state of awareness as he made his way down the empty hallway. The Institute was never busy but today it seemed to be particularly quiet. He could hear someone coughing behind one of the closed doors down a side hall. Rurrik looked in that direction, but the coughing abruptly ended.

The young Russian took the stairs to the second floor and then started down the central hall. This floor was quiet as well.

Somewhere water was running into a tub. As he turned the corner into the secondary hall, where his mother's room was, he froze. The door to her room stood open. It was the only open door in the hall. Rurrik checked behind himself and then crept toward the room. He looked in but did not enter. Inside the bed was made, the top of the bedside table bare, and the closet empty with its door standing open as well. His mother was gone.

A hand touched him on the shoulder. Rurrik spun and raised his arms in defense. Sonja Zagorsk, the duty nurse, recoiled and clutched her breast. "I'm sorry, Rurrik, I did not intend to scare you."

"Where is my mother?" Rurrik asked when the two had sufficiently recovered.

Nurse Zagorsk stepped forward and once again placed her hand on Rurrik's shoulder. "Your mother had another stroke. They took her to the hospital."

"My mother is in the hospital?"

"We tried to find you. Rurrik, your mother is dead. It was a major stroke this time. It happened yesterday, early in the morning. I am so sorry for your loss."

Rurrik was shocked but not surprised. He had expected this, just not today. He took a moment to compose himself but still, his words sounded like an echo in his own ears. "Thank you, Sonja. I will go to the hospital now."

Rurrik turned to leave but the nurse held onto his arm. "It is wrong for me to tell you this, but I feel I must," she spoke in a low voice. "Most of the people here have been abandoned by their families but you have been coming twice every week for nearly two years now. You are a good son."

"Thank you, Sonja. What is it you wish to tell me?"

"There were two men in earlier today. They were asking about your mother and, well, I think they were more interested in you. I also think they were KGB."

"It is but a small matter," Rurrik assured her.
Nurse Zagorsk released his arm and gave him a slight smile. "I believe they will be waiting for you at the hospital."

Rurrik waved off her concerns. "It is not a problem. I have been playing American Rock & Roll records again, that is all." He could not tell if she believed what he had told her. He was not sure he believed it himself. He decided to forgo his visit to the hospital. There was nothing he could do for his mother now.

The black sedan was gone from the parking place near the front of the institution. Rurrik checked every side street he passed on the way back to the bus stop, but the sedan was not to be seen. He caught the bus, transferred to a second, and then to a third before being deposited at the corner of Mira and Kulakov Street. The sun was long gone now, and the wind was back. It was seven long blocks down Kulakov Street to Rurrik's apartment and the wind grew sharper with each block. He knew this wind well. It was a wind that started in Siberia, crossed the Urals, and then the plains of central Russia. When it had built to maximum velocity and dropped to minimum temperature it hurtled over the Yausa River and up against Rurrik's coat. The coat was no match for the wind. Rurrik regretted being so hasty with his sleeve lining. If he had only saved it he might be able to reattach it in some manner. He could feel icy needles knifing through the buttonholes of his outer garment and then through the buttonholes of his shirt. He could even feel the wind through the eyelets of his worn boots.

A wind like this in April could be tolerated. In April, a Siberian wind would blow itself out before morning and then warmer air would start to filter in from the south. But this was October, not April. A wind such as this one that started in October could, potentially, blow without mercy for the next six months.

Rurrik hated the wind, and he hated the winter. He lowered his head and stuck his chin as far down in the collar of his coat as it would go. In the third block, a blast of cold air struck Rurrik so hard that it spun him around. As he waited for the gust to play itself out, he lifted his eyes and looked back toward Mira Street. A dark car, like a large black dog, seemed to be following his trail. It turned onto Kulakov Street, traveled half a block, killed its headlights, and rolled to a stop. Rurrik faced back into the wind and quickened his pace. Two blocks short of his apartment he turned to the south. One block south he turned back to the. He began to run. He glanced back over his shoulder. The black car was not to be seen. In two blocks he turned north, circling back to Kuakov Street.

When he neared the corner of Kulakov, he moved in tight against the apartment building on the west side of the street and eased up to the corner. The black sedan was just where he suspected it would be, parked halfway down the block, diagonally across from his apartment. Just beyond the parked car was one of the few working streetlights in this part of the city. Rurrik squatted down for a better viewing angle. From this position, he could see through the passenger compartment of the car. The sedan was empty.

Rurrik sprang straight up and did a pirouette all in one move. He landed softly and ran in a low crouch down the block, up a set of steps, and into the dark shadows of an unknown doorway. He leaned back against the door, sweating and shivering at the same time. Rurrik was one of the few Russians who did not smoke but he was beginning to regret that fact. He listened but heard nothing, only the wind.

The doorway was a good choice. A framework of wooden posts and scaffolding supported the deteriorating concrete arch above the door as it waited for repairs. The wood was gray and weathered, long streaks of rust bled from the nails. The wait for repairs had been a long one but the scaffolding worked to

Rurrik's advantage. The wooden posts reduced the visibility of anybody on the doorstep. After five minutes or so, Rurrik moved slowly to the edge of the darkness and, wrapping his arm around one of the posts, leaned out as far as he could and looked north toward Kulakov Street. There was nothing there. He looked to the south and saw only empty darkness.

Headlights flashed down the street. Rurrik pushed off of the scaffolding pole and swung back into the darkness of the doorway. He first felt the vibration in his feet and then heard the cracking. A fine dusting of sand and lime fell. And then, as if in slow motion, the massive concrete lintel above the doorway gave way. Rurrik, moving by animal instinct, bounded down the steps just ahead of the bouncing chunks of concrete. The cascade of rubble came to a stop at the bottom of the stairs. Rurrik, on the other hand, did not stop running until he reached the Kazan railroad station.

Just outside of the station he slowed to a walk, composed himself, and strolled into the building. The lobby was only sparsely populated. Rurrik mopped at the sweat that poured from his forehead and tried to act casual. He skirted the train platforms and ducked down a side hall. When he felt no eyes upon him, he slipped into the room which stored the misplaced baggage.

Rurrik scanned the baggage, focused on a comfortable-looking leather satchel, and picked it up as he passed. At the far end of the room was the janitor's closet. Rurrik opened the door and hastily rearranged the mops, brooms, and buckets. He closed the door, wedged a broom against the knob, and placing the satchel on the floor, sat down to wait for morning.

CHAPTER 5

At precisely 9:00 AM General Belov walked into his office and took his place in the large leather chair behind the carved wooden desk. At 9:01 AM the phone rang, and he picked up the receiver.

"General, Rurrik Zimas is on the line. He has called four times already," his secretary informed him.

"Yes, put him through," the general said as he leaned back in his chair. There was a sputtering, then a crackling, then what sounded like Rurrik talking in tongues from the bottom of a deep well. The line went dead. General Belov straightened up and hit the intercom button on his desk.

"Sorry, general," the secretary responded. "Let me try that line again."

Belov returned the receiver to the cradle and waited with his eyes on the phone. In short order, it rang again. This time it was Rurrik. "I've been thinking over your invitation to join you in the military," The young Russian spoke in as casual a manner as was possible for a man who had crouched all night in a broom closet. "This may be a good time for me to make some changes in my life."

"I heard about your mother," Belov confessed, "I was saddened by the news. Why don't you come by the office after the funeral and my secretary can start the paperwork needed to send you for preliminary training."

"Perhaps I could come by this morning," Rurrik countered. General Belov could sense the trepidation in the young man's voice. "This morning would be fine. In fact, you might want to stay with me for a few days. We could go together to the funeral."

***

Six weeks later, Private Rurrik Zimas sat once again in one of the wooden chairs in General Belov's office. His new brown uniform of coarse wool was an ill fit on his thin body. A woolen greatcoat, nearly as big as Rurrik himself, lay draped across the chair next to him. From time to time he glanced fondly at the coat and even went as far as to pat it gently.

"How do you like it now that you are a man in uniform?" Belov asked.

"I like it very much. The uniform is warm," Rurrik replied without a hint of sarcasm.

"I am glad you like the uniform, but you will no longer be needing it."

The former refusenik sat upright and put his arm out to shield the coat. "Am I out of the army so quickly?" Rurrik had become accustomed to regular meals and warm sleeping quarters. He was also more than a little curious about the special assignment the general had hinted at during their last meeting. For the first time in many years, Rurrik was optimistic about the future and now it seemed to be falling apart before him. "Listen, I can explain. That little incident during communications training. It was all a misunderstanding. I was only trying to listen to a little music, Rock & Roll music. How was a novice like myself to know the device used to jam Radio Free Europe was such a fragile thing? I only meant..."

"You must learn to be more careful," The general left his chair and, walking to the window, pulled the cord to close the heavy red drapes. When the drapes were shut, Belov stepped over to a small table against the wall. For the first time, Rurrik noticed the German-made movie projector.

"As I told you earlier, I have a special assignment for you. An assignment not suited to military dress. If you would, turn off the lights." The General said.

As Rurrik pushed the switch by the door he noticed the large silver-white screen on the adjacent wall. In the semi-darkness, he walked back to his chair and turned it to face the screen. Belov switched on the projector. It hummed and clicked with precision. "I want you to watch this and then we will talk."

Rurrik focused on the screen as the large numbers counted down to zero and the film began. The warm, dark room and the

soothing whirr of the projector had an immediate effect on
Rurrik, and he began to nod. No sooner had his chin nestled
against his chest when he was jolted awake by the clean chords
of a guitar playing a rock solo. It was coming from the newsreel
which turned out to be an American propaganda piece on the
evils of Rock & Roll.

There was a montage of images of Rock & Roll bands playing and American teenagers dancing. The musicians were
mostly black, and the teenagers were mostly white. The music
stopped abruptly. The soundtrack of the newsreel had been
crudely overdubbed. A voice in Russian explained what was
happening in the film. Rurrik looked at the American teenagers
with their exaggerated hairdos. He ran his hand across the short
buzz cut where his duck tails and hairworm had been.

A preacher was now on the screen speaking to his congregation from the pulpit. The Russian voice explained that the
preacher thought the music to be jungle music that was sent by
Satan to steal the souls of good Christian children. Rurrik
guessed the church was in the southern part of the United
States. The preacher and the congregation were sweating pro-
fusely. Next up was a shot of young black children picking cotton in an endless field and then a shot of a black neighborhood
in what appeared a major American city. It showed a seedy city
block with a bar, pool hall, and barbershop. A few Negro men

were lounging outside on the sidewalk. The voice-over explained that Rock & Roll evolved from the music of the former American slaves who were now the oppressed working class.

The last scene was of a politician giving a speech from behind his desk. Rurrik figured him to be the mayor of an American city. The Russian voice said that the politician would not allow Rock & Roll in his city because he knew it to be part of a plot between the Negroes and the communists to corrupt the youth of America. The film trailed off and ended. Belov turned off the projector and opened the drapes.

"Is that true?" Rurrik asked.

"Is what true?"

"Are we working to promote Rock & Roll in America?"

"No, no we are not. However, there are many here who believe that what is bad for America is good for the Soviet Union," the general explained. "It does not even sound like music to me, but if Rock & Roll will hasten the fall of the West then perhaps we should do what we can to see that Rock & Roll flourishes. We need to know more about this music, and toward that end, we need your help."

"You want me to teach you about Rock & Roll?" Rurrik asked in surprise.

General Belov smiled as he shook his head. He picked a folder from his desk. "What do you know of ships, merchant ships?"

"I have never been on a ship other than the ferry. I've seen the cargo ship unloading along the piers by the river," Rurrik offered.

"Never mind, you will have plenty of time to learn what you need to know on your way to America," the general said dismissively and then glanced over at his recent recruit. "Is something wrong, Rurrik? You look a bit pale."

Rurrik opened his mouth to reply and found he could not speak. He looked straight ahead; his face as blank as the movie screen before him.

Although Rurrik's next new uniform was gray, it was made of the same coarse fabric as the brown one and offered the same roomy fit. It was every bit as warm and easily deflected the cold wind that blew in from the Baltic Sea. General Belov had used the long train ride from Moscow to prepare Rurrik for his sea voyage.

How do you like your new uniform?" Belov asked as they walked along the pier. Rurrik labored beneath the weight of a stiff canvas sea bag while Belov carried only a swagger stick tucked under his arm.

"I believe gray is a better color for me," Rurrik replied as he stroked the lapel of his new greatcoat.

"I am an Army man myself but being in the Merchant Marines does have some advantages. The food is better, there is no mud, and you always sleep with a roof over your head. Of course, a member of the Merchant Marines must endure long months away from Mother Russia."

"Of course," Rurrik replied.

As they walked, they were followed by a soldier pushing a hand truck stacked with boxes. The entourage passed several large cargo ships and then stopped in front of a rather small, dingy freighter with the name Sabboto Noch painted on the bow. "Well, here we are. Let's get you aboard," Belov said. "We were lucky the port here in Leningrad was ice-free."

Rurrik looked over the ancient freighter. "Yes, lucky indeed."

Below deck, the freighter was every bit as dingy. The cabin that would be Rurrik's was small with several pipes crossing the ceiling below head height, but the bunk looked to be new and the smell of fresh paint hung in the air. It was the only refurbished part of the ship and Rurrik took that as a sign of the power commanded by the old general.

Rurrik and General Belov waited while the soldier carried the boxes from the hand truck and stowed them, as best he could, in the cabin. "Put that one on the bunk," Belov said to the soldier as he hefted the last box. The box was placed on the bunk and the soldier cut the packing seal. With his job completed the soldier stood at attention and snapped a sharp salute. Belov returned the salute and the soldier left.

Belov beckoned Rurrik into the cabin and shut the door. The general sat on the bunk, opened the box, and took out a large gray envelope with no markings. With the envelope removed Rurrik could now see that the box was filled with 45 rpm Rock & Roll records, their labels written in English.

"Your orders and instructions are in this envelope along with identification papers and a certain amount of American money," Belov was attempting to explain the situation to Rurrik but the young Russian was having a hard time keeping his eyes off the records in the box.

"Perhaps we should go over the plan once again," Belov said. "In six weeks you will dock at the port of New Orleans in the American South. You and the ship's first officer will go ashore. He will be reporting to the customs house, and you will be his escort. He will leave you alone briefly in the lobby of the customs house and you will go back out through the same door you entered. Three blocks to the north you will find the Federal Building. You will enter this building, find the proper office and tell him you are requesting political asylum. Are there any questions?"

"Are all these boxes full of records?" Rurrik asked.

"No, not all," Belov said as he pushed the lid closed on the opened box. "There are also Rock & Roll magazines and a record player as well, but there is much time for that later. For the present, it would be best if you focused on the information in the envelope. It will tell you what sort of things you will be looking for in America and where you will meet your contact to pass your information back to the Soviet Union. You must also learn as much as you can about sailing this ship."

Rurrik shifted around to get a better view of the record box. "Am I to sail the ship?"

"No, but you must be able to convince the Americans that you can." Belov also shifted his position to counter Rurrik's move. "You may find this hard to believe but the Soviet Union has had many defectors from our Merchant Marines."

"Yes, that is hard to understand."

The old general ignored the sarcasm in Rurrik's voice. "We have placed spies this way before. Sometimes we have been successful, sometimes not. Before the Americans accept your defection their CIA, similar to our KGB but far more sinister, will ask you many questions to determine if you are genuine. As he spoke Belov rose from the bunk, opened the door to the cabin, and looked out into the passageway. "In a case like this we first make a false KGB file and place it where the Americans can find it. This false file will contain documented incidents of anti-Soviet behavior to convince them that the defection is real."

Rurrik had taken advantage of the general's passageway recon mission and was now lifting the top records in the box to see what lay below. Belov returned and used his swagger stick to push down the records and close the box. "In your case, it was not necessary to falsify any documents. Your file speaks for itself." The General picked up the gray envelope from where Rurrik had discarded it on the bunk and pressed it into the younger man's hands. "Your instructions and your contacts are all in this envelope. You must memorize them before you get to New Orleans."

"Yes, and learn how to sail the ship."

"Most of all you must learn the ship. You will start your training in the morning. Get a good night's sleep and be on deck at 0600 hours." The old soldier embraced Rurrik. "Being a spy is a serious matter. You must be very careful in everything you do. And another thing you must remember, Plotkovic of the KGB is a small man, but his arms are extremely long. It is not beyond his capabilities to reach from Moscow to America." And with that, he was gone.

Belov was barely out of the door before Rurrik discarded the gray envelope and dove into the Rock & Roll records. As he was pulling them from the box, reading titles and sorting them into stacks, the general stuck his head back into the cabin. "If you are exposed by the CIA as a spy you will go to prison until Mother Russia can arrange an exchange for your release. I'm afraid you will be there a very, very long time."

When Belov had gone for the second and last time Rurrik returned the records to their box and closed the lid. He placed the box on top of the others. Sitting down on the bunk he picked up the gray envelope. Inside he found a small stack of official looking papers and a worn wallet containing a Merchant Marine identification card with his name and photo. It also contained a small amount of both Russian and American money. He dropped the wallet into his coat pocket and began to thumb through the papers. There were dozens of pages of maps, time-tables, code names, contacts, and instructions. He took the top page of the mission statement and, lying back on the bunk, began to read.

While there was some danger involved, Rurrik was sure this assignment would be one he could handle. Getting past the CIA screening would not be all that difficult. He would have to make them believe that he was thoroughly disgusted with the Soviet Union. That would be easy. Convincing them that he was a sailor would be the hard part, but it was highly unlikely they would take him out and make him sail a ship. He need only talk the talk, not walk the walk. As General Belov noted, there would be plenty of time to learn about ships on the long journey to America.

Once cleared by the Americans Rurrik would be free to go wherever he pleased. After all, that was the way things were done in America. There was the possibility that he would be watched by the American CIA but once they found out his interests were in Rock & Roll and not in rocket science their interest in him would wane. He knew nothing of who would contact him or when, but that matter was of small concern to Rurrik. He was being sent to America to wallow in Rock & Roll. The fact that he would, from time to time, be called upon to talk about it to a fellow Russian did not bother him.

In a short while, the sound of the ship's engines increased, and he felt the freighter begin to move. The sound and motion made him sleepy. He dropped the mission statement to the floor and took from his pocket the photo of Elvis and Sam Phillips in the cafe. This time he focused only on the girl serving the coffee. In a matter of minutes, he was asleep.

CHAPTER 6

At 6:00 AM the next morning Rurrik reported on deck to begin his education as instructed. It was still dark, and a cold wind blew icy needles of salt into his face. Karl, the young seaman assigned to teach Rurrik about the ship, did not seem to feel the cold. With exuberance, he began to explain how the ship was laid out. "Here on the foredeck, we have two hatches with a tabernacle in-between. The tabernacle holds the mast and four booms."

"Tabernacle and four brooms," Rurrik repeated but his words were lost to the wind. "Perhaps we should have some breakfast and talk about these things over coffee."

"Breakfast is served in the mess from 5:15 until 5:45," Karl explained.

The young seaman instructed Rurrik to follow him as he walked down towards the front of the ship. The wind was coming over the bow, colder than it had been amidships. Rurrik turned his back to Karl. He saw the light in the window of the door to the passageway which led below. Back in the bow, Karl was preoccupied sorting out a series of ropes. Rurrik left the young seaman to lecture the wind and went back down to his cabin.

Not only were his quarters warm, but they were also heaven. Rurrik rationalized that learning the ins and outs of being a member of the Soviet Merchant Marines was only half of the master plan for him during his weeks aboard the Sabboto Noch. The other half of the plan, the half Rurrik was born to, was to learn all he could about rock music. The boxes that shared the small cabin with him contained everything that Army Intelligence could gather on the musical phenomenon. There were fan magazines, sheet music, and photos of Rock & Roll stars. These were marvelous things indeed, but the best part was the components of a state-of-the-art, American HiFi and dozens of Rock & Roll records. He set up the system, stacked the changer with records, and climbed into bed.

On the floor near the bunk, he found the plain gray envelope which held the plans for his defection. At some point, he would have to memorize the details of these plans but right now the warmth of the cabin was making him too sleepy to concentrate. He put the gray envelope under his pillow and nodded off. In half an hour there was a pounding at the door. Rurrik got up, donned the blanket like a shroud, and opened the door.

"Seaman Zimas, you are to be on deck," the First Officer of the Sabboto Noch informed him.

Rurrik looked at the ice which clung to the First Officer's mustache. "Yes sir, I know. Believe me, I would like to be there, but I am working on an assignment for General Belov."

The First Officer glared at Rurrik wrapped in his blanket and then down at the HiFi. "And just what is the nature of that assignment?"

Rurrik produced the gray envelope and flashed it in front of the First Officer like a badge. "I am afraid that is a secret." The young seaman could tell by the older man's eyes that the First Officer recognized the envelope as emanating from a superior power to his own.

"I will try to be on deck by ten," the young mariner said as he closed the door and climbed back into bed.

It was only a few minutes past ten when Rurrik finally made his way back to the main deck. The sky was gray, but the wind had died down considerably. He found Karl, the young deck-hand who had tried earlier to teach him about the ship. The young man seemed bright and cheery despite having been at work for four hours now. "I love my work," Karl explained as he picked up the lecture right where he had left off earlier that morning.

He pointed out not only the boom but the gooseneck, the boom step, and the kingpin. He told Rurrik the difference between standing rigging and running rigging and how the topping lift and cargo whip were running rigging and worked off

61

the winch on the tabernacle. Karl pointed out the wheelhouse and the forecastle along with chocks, roller chocks, bitts, and fairleads. He corrected Rurrik when the Muscovite mistakenly referred to a davit as a miniature boom.

At first, it was somewhat interesting but, after about an hour, Rurrik's eyes began to glaze over. "Do you like American Rock & Roll music?" he asked to steer the subject away from ships and ship parts.

Karl looked around and pulled Rurrik behind the aft boom before he answered. "Yes, yes, I do. Are you a fan as well?"

The two continued to walk around the ship but now they talked not of hawsers and hatch coaming but of Carl Perkins and Big Mama Thornton. That evening Karl came to Rurrik's cabin with two of his friends, Peter the Lesser and Peter the Great. The two Peters worked in the engine room.

The four listened to Big Joe Turner sing *Shake Rattle and Roll* while they read about Bill Haley's London tour. During the days when the weather was less than horrid, Rurrik and Karl walked around the deck talking about Rock & Roll. When they were in the vicinity of the ship's First Officer they talked of freighters and freight. When the weather was bad, which it often was, Rurrik and Karl hung out with the two Peters in the engine room. Rurrik liked the engines and the heat they produced. He also enjoyed the company of the genuine Merchant Marines.

The Sabboto Noch picked its way through the many passages between the islands east of Denmark. Rurrik and his small band listened to Garnet Mims while memorizing the words to Chuck Berry's *Maybellene*. The ship crossed the North Sea and steamed into the open Atlantic. Rurrik stuck a publicity photo of Elvis Presley on the wall of his cabin and the friends tried to comb their short hair to match the photo. They lip-synced as they listened to Fats Domino sing *Blue Monday*. Some nights the four would gather in the steel stairwell to sing doo-wop.

In the back of his mind, Rurrik knew he would need a working knowledge of the ship if he was going to convince the CIA his defection was legitimate. Despite his mission being as innocuous as Rock & Roll, he could not imagine it would go well if he were to be exposed as a Russian spy. The Americans would put him in prison for life. The only way out would be through some sort of prisoner exchange and that would only work if the Russians wanted Rurrik back. He was fairly sure they would not. And yet, all this talk about freight and freighters bored him to tears and the pages from the gray envelope lay hopelessly buried in his cabin beneath an avalanche of records and music magazines.

The ship skirted the British Isles, crossed the North Atlantic, and turned to the south. The weather improved now. Rurrik spent more time on deck with Karl, but he still could not get his mind around all the many ship parts and functions. The First Officer had long given up on the thought of getting any work out of Rurrik.

The freighter sailed south along the coast of North America, around the tip of Florida, and into the Gulf of Mexico. The weather was more than warm now, it was hot. Rurrik had never known weather like this. It melted away all the memories of cold Moscow winters, cold-hearted Moscow police, and shadowy figures in heavy coats. He thought about his mother often but did not mourn her passing. She had been dead only a matter of months, but she had been gone from him since her first stroke nearly three years earlier.

Things changed even more dramatically when the ship entered the mouth of the Mississippi River. Even in January, the vegetation along the river's banks was a lush green by Moscow standards. Here, to the north, were the remains of a stone fort and then, a little further on, more remains on the opposite bank. Fish jumped in the brown water and a flock of pelicans flew escort to the freighter. At one point the Sabboto Noch came in close to the riverbank and Rurrik saw an alligator the size of a sofa sunning itself on a mud flat. He thought it to be the kind of creature that myth was made of.

Ships were everywhere in this part of the Mississippi. Local fishing boats mixed with freighters, tankers, and ocean-going barges from every part of the world. More ships than Rurrik ever dreamed possible. He noticed that the ships from the Soviet Union and the Eastern Bloc tended to be the shabbiest, but few were as shabby as the Sabboto Noch.

As the afternoon shadows lengthened the old freighter was overtaken by a ship of the American Navy. The warship towered over Rurrik as he stood at the railing on the port side of the Sabboto Noch. The sun, low on the western horizon, lent fire to the polished brass and fresh paint of the American ship. The young Russian could feel the vibrations from the war ship's powerful engines.

A small covey of officers was gathered near the railing on the American ship. They were looking toward the west and shading their eyes against the sun. One of them turned and looked toward the Sabboto Noch. The American officer pointed in the direction of the Soviet freighter and drew the group's attention to the small craft. Although there were more than fifty yards between the two ships, Rurrik was sure the men on the American warship were looking right at him, sure they knew his secret. He pulled the shirt collar up around his face, scurried behind the aft boom, and flattened himself against the wall.

The young mariner was now facing north and could see dozens of ships waiting at anchor. To the west was the city of New Orleans rising above the levee. Lights were beginning to blink on. The city was not as large as Moscow but certainly, it was large enough to hide a man, Rurrik reassured himself.

With all these ships, coming and going, a strange face in New Orleans would not be seen as a novelty. He relaxed and began to count the waiting ships. One of the closest freighters at anchor was also from the Soviet Union. Two men, one tall and the other squat stood at the railing. Rurrik waved and stepped forward, but his view of the other Soviet ship was blocked by the sail of a luxury yacht as it glided between the two freighters. When the yacht had passed the two men were gone. Rurrik remembered what General Belov had told him about Colonel Plotkovic's long reach, a reach that could extend even to America. He ducked back down the hatch that led below deck.

Back in his small cabin the young Russian sat on the bunk and tried to get his breathing under control. There was precious little time left to learn all he would need to know about his upcoming defection. He could hear the engines being shifted into reverse and feel the ship beginning to slow. The freighter would soon be coming to anchor to await its turn to dock along the New Orleans waterfront. All was not lost. Surely this ship would not dock right away. There were dozens of freighters awaiting their turn and most were larger than the Sabboto Noch, much larger. It might be a day or two before a berth opened for his little freighter and Rurrik could use that time to study the information in the gray envelope. But where was it?

He jumped to his feet and began a frantic search for the packet and the papers it once contained. The envelope itself was pushed back under his bunk. Unfortunately, it contained only a few sheets of paper and those were badly stained by coffee. The young mariner heard the anchor being lowered. With both hands, Rurrik scooped 45 records and Rock & Roll magazines back into the boxes and uncovered more official paperwork. When he believed most pages had been recovered, he sat on his bunk and began to sort through them. There was still tonight and probably most of tomorrow or even more time if he was lucky. In the ballet academy and later in auto mechanics school Rurrik had always been known as a quick study. Surely, he could, given a day or two, learn what he needed to know in order to keep from being sent to some American gulag.

Most of the papers were accounted for but the maps were missing. Rurrik remembered that Karl and Peter the Great had taped them together and then fastened them to the wall. They had been using a red pen to plot the birthplaces of Rock & Roll icons. The maps were still there, right behind him on the wall above the bunk.

From Chuck Berry's birthplace in Saint Louis to Fats Domino's in New Orleans, from Buddy Holly in Texas to Little Richard in Georgia, a series of red dots spread across the American south and up and down the Mississippi River. Rurrik stopped to study the pattern the dots made on the map. He found the red pen amid the litter on the floor and drew a line connecting the outermost dots. It formed an elongated circle. In an uncharacteristic show of Russian pride, he drew a small Sputnik traveling the ellipse. In the center of the ellipse, he drew a circle representing the earth. Rurrik was surprised to find that at the very center of the circle representing the earth was Memphis, Tennessee.

Rurrik pulled the photo of Elvis and Sam Phillips from his pocket and read the caption. *Elvis and Sam Phillips relax at Taylor's Cafe next door to Sun Records in Memphis, Tennessee,* it read. He looked, once again, at the Asian-American waitress and wondered how long ago the photo had been taken and how far it was from New Orleans to Memphis. Rurrik's thoughts were interrupted by a pounding on his door. He quickly folded the photo, returned it to his pocket, tore the maps from the wall, and hastily stuffed them into the gray envelope.

Rurrik opened the door to find the First Officer standing there with a gray envelope of his own. The older man looked in past Rurrik at the mass of clutter that covered the floor, bunk, and walls of the small cabin. Next, he looked at the stained and tattered envelope in Rurrik's hands. "Comrade Zimas, I see you have your orders."

"Yes, First Officer, I was just doing some review." Rurrik brushed lint and breadcrumbs from the envelope.

"Let us review together," the First Officer said. "In the morning we will dock in New Orleans. You, Seaman Zimas, will be assigned to accompany me on a mission to the U.S.

Customs House at the corner of Canal Street and Decatur Street. I will leave you in the lobby of the building while I go upstairs with the ship's bill of lading. When I have gone you will leave the Customs House by the Canal Street exit, turn north, and walk three blocks to the Federal Building. There, at the office of immigration, you will present yourself and explain that you seek asylum."

"Yes sir, The Federal Building at Canal and Decatur. It is all here in my envelope and in my mind as well." Rurrik made a feeble attempt to straighten some of the papers in his envelope and nearly dropped them. He smiled thinly and touched a finger to the side of his head.

"The Customs house is on Decatur; the Federal Building is on Chartres. Never mind, you will just need to remember to walk to the north, three blocks." The First Officer held three fingers up in front of Rurrik's face.

"Yes, yes, of course, Decatur, that is what I meant to say," Rurrik replied. "I have memorized the plan. It is foolproof."

"I have found fools to be far more industrious and resourceful than one might think when it comes to foiling well-made plans," the First officer said. "Once you are in the hands of the Americans you will be on your own. For your sake, I hope you have learned enough about the Merchant Marines to fool the American CIA."

"Yes sir," Rurrik said without conviction. "I have been learning every day."

"You are a lucky man to be able to learn so much by osmosis," the First Officer extended his hand. "I will need your gray envelope."

"I will bring it to you the very first thing in the morning."

The First Officer took hold of Rurrik's envelope. "This must be destroyed before we dock." Rurrik held tightly to his end of the envelope while the First officer tried to tug it free. Rurrik resisted but the First Officer glared at the young seaman. Rurrik withered and relinquished the envelope.

When the First Officer had gone Rurrik returned to his bunk. This time he sat with his back against the wall and his knees pulled up against his chest. He held that position for a long time and then when darkness was full and the ship was quiet, he made his move.

Rurrik found his sea bag and emptied it onto his bunk. He dug through the wadded-up clothes and selected a black sweater, dark gray pants, and canvas shoes. He sorted through the records, picked out the best, and, wrapping them in the greatcoat, stuffed them into the sea bag. He donned the black sweater and gray pants, hefted the sea bag, and left the cabin locking the door behind him. Above deck he found Karl standing night watch on the forecastle. Rurrik handed the key to his cabin to his friend. "The records and Hi-fi are yours. It might be wise to get what you want before morning," he said.

Quietly Rurrik made his way to the stern. The night was starless, and the cool air hung heavy over the water. To the west, the city of New Orleans projected a neon glow up and onto the low cover of clouds. It might be smaller than Moscow, but it was much brighter and more colorful. It called to him with a Siren's song. Rurrik figured it to be about half a mile from the ship to the levee in front of the city. Too far even for a strong swimmer and Rurrik was not a strong swimmer. To the best of his knowledge, he was not a swimmer at all. He did not know for sure that he could not swim, it was just that he had never tried.

Despite the darkness, Rurrik could make out the silhouette of trees along the riverbank to the north. In that direction, it appeared to be about two or three hundred yards from the Sabboto Noch to the shore. Surely even a non-swimmer, if provided with a floatation device, could make two hundred yards. The distance mattered little to the young Russian. Death by drowning seemed superior to life in an American prison.

The young mariner removed a life preserver from the row along the railing and flexed it for strength. It split down the middle. A second one crumbled like sawdust as he tried to untie it. The third one, the one he got from the bulkhead, felt light and buoyant and did not break apart in his hands. Rurrik tied the bag to the life preserver and the life preserver to his leg with a bit of rope and then, hoisting the over-stuffed duffel to his shoulder, climbed onto the railing. He took a deep breath and looked down at the dark muddy water below him. The air was colder than he anticipated, and a chill ran through his body.

A night bird called from somewhere near the ship and a second bird answered from the direction of the shore. The sound of violent splashing came from the riverbank. The bird near the ship called once again but no response came. Rurrik looked off into the black bayou night and thought of the alligator he had seen earlier in the day. The bird near the ship called and then called again. There was no answer.

Rurrik climbed down from the railing, untied the life preserver, and threw it as far as he could out over the dark river. Dragging his canvas bag behind him, he retrieved the key from Karl and returned to his cabin.

The young Russian lay on his bunk with his hand folded behind his head. He would still have tomorrow and perhaps another day before the ship moved from its anchor position into one of the berths along the waterfront of New Orleans. In Russia, there were always delays. There was still time to plan an escape. He would look things over in the morning but for now, the best thing to do was to get some sleep. He closed his eyes and listened to the familiar sounds of the ship. What he heard was the anchor chain starting its wind. In a matter of minutes, the engines revved, and the ship began to rock softly back and forth as it moved in the direction of the city. Rurrik stared up toward the pipes that crossed above his bunk. His eyes were unfocused.

Chapter 7

It was morning and Rurrik dressed as if he was going to his own execution. For all he knew, he was. The First Officer would escort him to the Customs House but after that, the plan was a bit vague in the young mariner's mind. He remembered that the Federal Building was where he had to go and that it was but a few blocks from the Customs House, but he wasn't sure in what direction. He wasn't even sure what the Federal Building was or just which office he was to look for when he got there.

He had learned a little about ships and shipping from Karl and the two Peters from the engine room, Peter the Lesser and Peter the Great, but he was sure it would not be enough to convince even the greenest CIA operative that he was indeed a member of the Soviet Merchant Marines and not a Russian spy. Even if he did somehow survive the ordeal that awaited him at the Federal Building, he would never manage to reunite with his ship, the Sabboto Noch. Somewhere in that gray envelope, such a reunion was mentioned. He could not remember when and where that rendezvous was to take place and the gray envelope was now gone. A life at hard labor in an American prison camp was the best he could hope for.

Rurrik found his cap and tried to work it back into its original shape. For the first time, he polished his shoes and his brass. He brushed his dress uniform and his heavy wool greatcoat. The young Russian looked one last time at the photo of Elvis and Sam Phillips drinking coffee in Taylor's cafe. He lightly kissed the young waitress who was serving them and folded the photo lovingly into his pocket.

When he was ready, he reported to the First Officer who waited on deck in the cool, misty, January morning air. The two walked in silence down the gangplank and through the shipping yards toward the main exit from the docks. Rurrik looked back at the old, rusting freighter that had been his home for the last few weeks. The First Officer showed his papers at the guard house, and they passed through the main gate and out into the city of New Orleans. The sun melted away the mist and Rurrik began to regret wearing the greatcoat. By the time the two seamen reached the Customs House he was beginning to perspire, cold beads trickled down his back. He loosened the top two buttons which offered some relief but not all of his discomfort could be blamed on the coat.

They entered the Customs House from Canal Street and stopped in the lobby. Rurrik's face felt cold and yet sweat ran down into his collar.

"You will wait here," The First Officer instructed in a voice that sounded very distant and very loud at the same time.

Rurrik's head felt light. He looked toward the First Officer. The man stepped closer and said in a harsh whisper, "Back out the door we entered through, turn right, to the north, three blocks, the Federal Building. It is where you will defect."

The young mariner looked around the symmetrical lobby trying to get his bearings. There were two identical doors, and two identical sets of stairs. He turned back to the First Officer, but the man was already halfway up one set of marble steps to the second floor. On uncertain legs, Rurrik walked over to a bench against the wall, took off his greatcoat, and sat down. The young Russian leaned back and felt the coolness of the marble which began, in turn, to cool his blood. His head cleared and in a short while, he could once again try to stand on his feet. Rurrik stood, shivered, and picked up his greatcoat. He looked at the two identical doors and thought that there was something familiar about the door to his right. He sat back down to study it. There was something about the outside shadows he could see through the glass. They looked like eastern shadows, and that would mean the sun was in the west. Somehow that didn't seem right. Perhaps they were western shadows and, if they were, that could only mean…

"Can I help you?" The voice sounded loud in his ear. Rurrik turned to see a tall, muscular man standing next to the bench. The man wore a blue-gray uniform.

The young mariner sprang to his feet and snapped a salute. "No sir," Rurrik said with authority. He threw his greatcoat over his shoulder, spun sharply on his heels, and strode with determination toward the exit with the somewhat familiar shadows.

The bewildered postal employee watched as Rurrik marched out through the Decatur Street exit and, after looking in both directions, picked one, and set off with long determined steps.

The sidewalks were filled with people in, what seemed to Rurrik, exotic dress. Men in vanilla-colored suits with pastel shirts, contrasting neckties, and Panama hats. Women sported flowered frocks in every color of the rainbow and hats that defied description. The men and women themselves showed more variation of skin color than Rurrik ever dreamed possible. Skin like copper and skin like brass, chocolate, vanilla, coffee black, and coffee with cream; colored skin was everywhere. Nowhere, however, could he see, despite his months on the open seas, skin as white as his.

After several blocks, the young Russian found a bench and sat, watching the people with fascination. He remembered that the Federal building was within a few blocks but could not recall how many. For some reason, the direction north stuck in his mind. He sat for a long time in a state of suspended animation and then, getting back up, looked both ways, up and down the street. Neither the Customs House nor the Federal Building could be seen.

Rurrik took off his hat and let the sun bathe his face. He had to, once again, pick a direction. The sun felt good on his face. That was the direction he chose.

It was late morning now. One might think that an experienced sailor would know that a man walking with the sun on his face was not walking north. Rurrik was not burdened by such enlightenment. And yet, despite his inexperience, he might have noticed the misdirection if he had not been so overwhelmed by all the new things he was seeing. The street was filled with cars; big American cars with sensual chrome bumpers and rocket-like tail fins motored in both directions and filled the parking spaces. And these cars were not all black, they were coral, turquoise, lemon, lime, and sky blue. Rurrik even saw several cars that were painted with two different colors.

It was not just the automobiles, everywhere he beheld a tapestry of color, pattern, and texture. What in Moscow had been flat, gray concrete was, here in New Orleans, all an assembly of wood, brick, stucco, wrought iron railings, cast iron grill work, canvas awning, tin, glass, and stone. Quoins and pillars, brackets and parapets, doors and windows of every shade with sills, lintels, fanlight transoms, and shutters of every hue lined both sides of the street. And everywhere were signs; signs in all the colors of the rainbow and mostly all in English. From the Rock

& Roll magazines, Rurrik had learned to read a good deal of the language and now he would have to put that knowledge to use. He would find the Federal Building and let the fates take it from there. It was easier than he thought. Two blocks down and across the street, he saw a building with Federal written on the awning above the wide double doors.

The Federal Iron Works first opened for business in 1863 during the Union Army's occupation of New Orleans. They made a good living during the war by doing some of the finer iron work for the forces of occupation. Fifteen years later, when the Union occupation finally ended, things could have gone badly for the firm. The people of New Orleans hated General Butler and his army of occupation. They could have frozen the iron works out of business in short order. What saved the company was that the city's love of fine craftsmanship neutralized its hatred of the Union Army.

The city tolerated the iron works because they needed it but, in seventy-five some-odd years, they never warmed to the establishment. Over time, sons followed their fathers into the business and inherited skills in the craft along with the city's disdain. As a result, the men who were employed by Federal Iron Works were very businesslike but not overly friendly. In short, they did not suffer fools gladly. When Rurrik walked into the workshop and tried to defect amid the welders, chop saws, and workbenches they made short work of the situation. He quickly found himself back on the sidewalk. His greatcoat landed beside him. The young Russian's Soviet Merchant Marine hat had not followed him out through the door, but he knew better than to try to reenter the iron works and retrieve it.

Rurrik's luck did not improve much at the Federal Bank on the corner of Decatur and Toulouse. He was not forcibly ejected from the bank but, when he noticed the clerk he was trying to communicate with was, in turn, trying to get the eye of the security guard, he withdrew from the field. It was in the Federal Pawnshop, across from the French Market, that Rurrik got his first friendly reception.

Rurrik entered the building with reservations. Something did not seem very official about the long room with the high ceiling in which he found himself. Shafts of bright sunlight cut in through the windows overpowering the small bulbs which hung from the rafters. Motes of dust played in the beams.

To the right were bins of used and misused power tools along with shelves of radios and televisions. On the left were a set of shelves crowded with worn kitchen appliances. Fishing rods and golf clubs shared cardboard barrels with curtain rods and baseball bats. At the far end of the room, Max Baeder, a short, middle-aged man, sat behind a glass case filled with jewelry, watches, and cameras. A screen of wire mesh shielded him from the toasters, Philcos, four irons, and customers. Max did not look up from his newspaper until Rurrik stood in front of the small conversation port hole in the wire mesh.

"What can I do for you, Admiral?" the pawnbroker said as he knocked nonexistent ash from an unlit cigar.

Rurrik fingered the metal insignia on the collar of his coat. "But I am not an admiral,"

"Sorry, but don't I detect the aroma of damp wool and the sea?"

The young Russian came to attention. "I am in the Soviet Merchant Marines, and I wish to defect,"

"Defect? Not in here you don't. The restroom is for customers only," Max said with a laugh.

"Say, is that a Russian Navy greatcoat?"

"Merchant Marines," Rurrik corrected.

"Coat-wise it's about the same thing. I can let you have ten dollars for it."

Rurrik clutched the coat defensively. The weather in New Orleans was far too warm for such a serious coat, but every Russian knows the winter will come again. "No thank you."

"I could go as high as fifteen if you can get those iron filings off. Might be nice to have a little folding money in your pocket."

"Perhaps I will come back to see you when my defection is over."

"We don't get many disenchanted Soviets in this part of town. For the most part, they hang out down on the waterfront and up around the Federal Building," Max said.

"I would like very much to find the Federal Building."

Max pointed in the direction of the door. "West on Decatur until you hail Canal Street; hard to starboard and hold her steady for about two blocks."

Rurrik pointed to the east. "West on Decatur."

Maxie pointed in the opposite direction. "To the west, Admiral. The direction the sun sets in. Works the same here as it does in Russia, I would imagine. And if you change your mind about that coat, come back and see me."

Rurrik stood on the steps of Federal Pawn and looked toward the west. The sun was not yet setting, but it was past its zenith. The young Russian felt tired and, folding his greatcoat for a cushion, sat down to rest. Most of the people on Decatur Street were tourists who paid little attention to him. The afternoon shadows were growing, and the aroma of food emanated from the nearby French Market. Rurrik had not eaten since dinner the night before. He got up, shouldered his coat, and crossed the street. At the end of the block was the entrance to the market in the form of a scale replica of Napoleon's Arc de Triomphe. Rurrik passed under it and into a world of food no Russian could ever have imagined.

In Moscow's markets, the food was mostly white. White potatoes, green-white cabbage, and purple-white turnips were, here and there, punctuated with dark red beets and dark brown bread. The small booths and kiosks that made up the French Market were ablaze with color. Brilliant oranges, apples, and bananas competed with bright green peppers, cucumbers, and broccoli. Braids of garlic, onions, and chili peppers hung like curtains. There were towers of fresh bread, rolls, and pastries and bins of peanuts, walnuts, and pecans, in the shell and out. Fish, crabs, oysters, and shrimp overflowed tubs of ice. Rurrik walked in a trance.

A black woman in a floral dress and a large straw hat sat at a table behind a waterfall of dried peppers. The table held dozens of small bottles of red and green colored sauce. The bright labels sported everything from pictures of peppers and tropical birds to little red devils. All around the woman were wooden crates with pepper sauce labels. Rurrik leaned over to admire one of the labels. It was green and featured two parrots, one red, one yellow, flanking a pepper that looked like a small apple. "Child, do you like your food hot?" the woman asked as she removed a white cracker from a paper sleeve.

Rurrik thought of many nights sitting in his cold Moscow apartment eating cold potato soup.

"Yes, yes I do, very much."

The woman sorted through the open bottles on the table and found one with the two parrots on the label. She placed a drop of the sauce on the cracker and offered it to Rurrik. "Be careful now, these habaneras is serious."

The Muscovite held the cracker and watched the drop as it soaked in. It did not look hot. He held his finger just above it. It did not feel hot. He popped the cracker into his mouth and began to chew. At first, he tasted nothing but the white cracker and vinegar, and then the heat wave began to build. It started at the back of his tongue and spread to the roof of his mouth. Next, the sides of his tongue ignited like he had a mouthful of red-hot pins. He stuck out his tongue and fanned it with his hand but that only succeeded in spreading the pain to his lips. The skin felt like it was burning off. Rurrik's eyes began to water.

The woman in the floral dress read the young mariner's signs of distress and hurried to his aid. She took hold of his hand and led him to a place where a galvanized tub held chopped ice covered with shrimp the size of hockey pucks. She grabbed a large chunk of ice and held it against Rurrik's mouth. The woman took off her straw sun bonnet and fanned him. The young Russian nodded his appreciation but when he removed the ice to speak the pain returned. The woman pushed the ice back against Rurrik's mouth. "You best stick to grits," she advised.

When he had recovered from his ordeal enough to be able to talk, he thanked the woman again and resumed his wandering through the marketplace. He marveled at all he saw and occasionally filched ice from one of the seafood stands. In about twenty minutes the burning sensation on his lips and in his mouth was all but gone. He could not help but notice that his sinuses were clear, and his sense of smell seemed to be more acute than it had ever been. The aroma of food was making him dizzy.

The most alluring smell was coming from a small booth that featured take-out food. The menu was written on the slats of a lime green shutter beside the service window. Rurrik looked for words he could recognize among the offerings. He passed up etouffee, jambalaya, and gumbo. They might be wonderful, or they might not be food at all. Or, worse yet, they might be made with small, apple-shaped peppers. He had no way of knowing. Near the bottom of the menu shutter, he found red beans and rice. Not only did he know what rice and beans were he knew them to be filling and the price was right. For a dollar, he got a large cardboard container of the entree, a plastic spoon, half a loaf of French bread, and a Coca-Cola. The woman behind the counter held up a brightly colored bottle of hot sauce and offered to lace Rurrik's rice and beans. He declined the offer.

The young mariner returned to the pawn shop steps to eat. He again folded his greatcoat for a cushion, sat down, and opened the container. The red beans and rice looked like nothing he had ever seen before. He stirred them with the plastic spoon. Chunks of andouille sausage rolled to the surface; more meaty sausage than he would have seen in a week aboard the Sabboto Noch. Cautiously he took a tiny amount of the gravy on the spoon. He touched it to the tip of his tongue and waited for the pain. It did not come.

The young Muscovite put a large spoonful of beans and rice into his mouth and then another and another. With the fourth scoop, he held the spoon in position, leaned back, and looked down the street. A woman stood out on an iron second-story balcony turning over the soil in a flower box with a hand trowel. Just a few months ago he was facing down the barrel of a Russian winter and now here he was looking forward to a Southern spring. Events had picked him up like a wave, transported him across the ocean, and dropped him on this step. At some point, he would have to try to find the Federal Building and get on with his mission of defection, but for right now he chose to ignore that part of his life. He finished his meal, leaned against the railing, closed his eyes, and began to hum *Walkin' to New Orleans*.

CHAPTER 8

"You a fan of the fat man, are you?"

The voice broke Rurrik's trance. He was no longer alone on the steps of Federal Pawn. Two others had joined him.

Gizmo Broussard had lived it and loved it all; jazz, blues, rhythm and blues, rockabilly, and Rock & Roll. As a teenager, he once played upright bass behind Louie Armstrong and drums behind Son House when the Delta Bluesman was still known as Eddie James. He played keyboard with the in-house band at Cosimo Matassa's J&M Studios and filled in on rhythm guitar for Louis Jordan when the band leader came to town one musician short. Gizmo played lead guitar for Roy Brown when Roy made his recording of "Good Rockin' Tonight." Now approaching sixty, he had a musical resume few white men could equal. Gizmo's companion, Prince Albert, although still shy of his eleventh birthday could claim a lifetime of musical experience as well. His black skin shone like the knees and elbows of his worn tuxedo.

"Mind if we join you?" The older man asked. His voice was like a rusty winch.

"You are welcome," Rurrik replied as he extended his nearly empty container of red beans and rice. "You would like?"

"Thank you for asking but...eh...no thanks. We just ate," Gizmo replied to Rurrik and then turned to the young man who accompanied him. "Prince Albert, would you mind going in and getting my guitar from ole Maxie?" The Prince danced up the steps like Astaire, danced back down, and then up and into the pawn shop.

"You're new to the Quarter, aren't you?" Gizmo said.

"I am from Moscow. Is in the Soviet Union," Rurrik explained.

"No kidding," Gizmo replied with a touch of sarcasm. "I love the smell of the open sea. You wouldn't happen to be a navy man, would you?"

"Merchant Marines," Rurrik corrected.

"We don't get many mariners down here in the Quarter. We're quite a ways from the waterfront." Gizmo said.

"I am looking for Federal Building. I could not find."

Gizmo looked up toward the Federal Pawn sign that swung above their heads. "Well, you were close."

"My name is Rurrik Zimas," Rurrik stated as he held out his hand.

"Gizmo Broussard," the older man said as they shook. The Prince returned with the guitar. "And this young man is my protégé, Prince Albert," Gizmo continued. "He got his name off of a can."

90

The black child handed the instrument to Gizmo, bounced over to shake Rurrik's hand, and bowed deeply.

"Glad to met you," Rurrik smiled

"He don't talk," Gizmo pointed out.

Rurrik bowed toward Prince Albert and then focused his attention on Gizmo's guitar. "Do you play Rock & Roll music?"

In answer to the question Gizmo ran through a rocking guitar solo. Rurrik was frozen in admiration. "I know that song. That is beginning of '*Johnny B. Goode*' by the Rock & Roll hero, Chuck Berry."

"In fact, Berry took it from an old Louis Jordan tune called '*Ain't That Just Like a Woman*'," Gizmo explained as he tightened one of his strings.

"I do not know that song," the young mariner said with regret.

Gizmo strummed the guitar and made a few more adjustments to the strings. "I don't believe I know it anymore either. Everybody wants the Berry tune anyway. Would you like to hear '*Johnny B. Goode*'? That one I do know."

The old musician started the song from the top. Prince Albert placed the open guitar case on the lowest step and dance out onto the sidewalk. By now it was late afternoon, quitting time, and the sidewalks of the quarter were beginning to fill as office workers joined the tourists. A small crowd gathered around the steps. Gizmo made the guitar ring and Albert moved as if his body were wired to the strings. Rurrik felt the beat and began to tap his feet and rock back and forth on his greatcoat. Albert smiled at the young Russian, grabbed him by the hands and pulled him to his feet.

The would-be defector looked back at his greatcoat folded on the step and then hesitantly joined the black youth. He did his best to keep up with the younger dancer. Albert swiveled his hips and slid sideways using only his heels and toes for propulsion. Rurrik did the same. The boy in the tux spread his legs and hopped forward pumping his arms in an exaggerated motion. The athletic Russian followed right behind him. Albert pranced like a pony holding his arms low. Rurrik followed suit. At the end of the run, Rurrik took the lead, dropped into the Chuck Berry duck walk, and bounced along the sidewalk. Albert fell in line. As the song ended the two leapt into the air and landed in a split.

Rurrik felt good. Better than he had in a long, long time; better, he thought, then he had ever felt in his life. The young Russian had been so lost in the music and the dance that he hadn't noticed that the crowd, gathered around the street performers, now filled the sidewalk. Not only were the people clapping but they were showering coins into the guitar case as well. Gizmo struck up another tune and then another. The dancers kept pace with the driving guitar, sometimes dancing in unison and sometimes in opposition. The crowd grew and so did the pile of coins in the instrument case.

After nearly two hours the three troubadours were exhausted, and the guitar case was heavy with coins. Rurrik and Gizmo rested while Prince Albert counted the money.

"How much today?" Gizmo asked

Prince Albert tapped out a code with his foot, heel and toe.

"A shade past twelve dollars," Gizmo translated. "I thought it sounded big but that's our best yet, and this is a weeknight. Let's see, that's two dollars for Maxie and five for each of us."

Prince Albert popped up and down tapping his ring on the metal railing of the steps and pointing at Rurrik.

Gizmo laughed and rocked back and forth. "All right, three-way split. Take that pile into the Federal, pay Maxie, and get us some folding money. And take the guitar back while you're at it, if you will"

"Don't you own one guitar?" Rurrik asked in disbelief.

"Sure, I do, I own that one and it's a beauty. I had to hock it a while back. Cash flow problem. Maxie lets me take it out, sort of on loan, to do some fund raisin'. We're paying him back in installments," Gizmo explained. "Look, there ain't many hoofers can keep pace with Prince Albert, how would you like to join our little troupe? We do one show most every night and a matinee on Saturday. Maxie won't let us take the guitar off the steps, but we've played worse corners."

"Could you teach to me Rock & Roll?" Rurrik asked.

"Teach you Rock & Roll? Well, I don't know. Rock & Roll ain't something to be learned. It don't come from the brain like the classical music of Europe or your country. Rock & Roll comes from the heart and the guts and some of the lower regions of the body. I'm an old Blues man so the transition was easy for me. Either you have Rock & Roll inside of you or you don't. First impressions tell me that you do. Either way, you stay with us, and you'll catch on. We're not exactly the Russian Navy but we do have our moments."

"I would like that but first I have to find proper authorities and defect," Rurrik explained.

"Defect! Whoa now. Don't go doing nothin' rash on our account,"

"Is not because of you. I have come to this country to be free."

"Of course, you were lookin' for the Federal Building, weren't you?"

"Yes, I should go there at once."

"You certainly should but it's closed now. Tell you what; we'll go by there first thing in the morning. Get you properly defected and all."

Prince Albert returned with a small wad of bills and handed them to his partner.

"What now my friend?" Gizmo asked Prince Albert.

Prince Albert rubbed his stomach.

Gizmo divided up the money. "Why dinner, of course. And then what?"

Prince Albert puffed out his cheeks, pushed his small belly out as far as it would go, and played an invisible piano.

"Go see Fats. Excellent idea my young friend."

Albert pointed at Rurrik and did his piano imitation once again.

The old Musician handed folded money to the young Russian. "Sure, Rurrik will go with us. No student of Rock & Roll would pass up a chance to see Fats Domino."

"We will go see Fats Domino? He is one of the true heroes of Rock & Roll," Rurrik stuttered.

"Soon as we eat."

Rurrik, Gizmo and Prince Albert crossed the street to the market and got dinner. Rurrik once again ordered the red beans and rice and declined the hot sauce. They returned to the steps of Federal Pawn and ate.

When they were finished with their meal the three walked to the corner and started up Ursulines Street. The evening was warm for January, but a light mist hung in the air condensing on the car hoods and the metal gratings of the sidewalk. By the time the trio turned west on Bourbon the mist could be officially classified as rain. Rurrik held his greatcoat aloft and made a tent to shield Prince Albert and himself.

After several blocks, Rurrik looked up to see the marquee for Tambura Hall, its bright lights reflecting off the wet street. Fats Domino's name was written on the marquee in big block letters. Outside the double doors, a large crowd filled the sidewalk and spilled into the street.

Rurrik stopped and viewed the sight with disappointment. He had seen many lines in the Soviet Union; lines for bread, lines for clothes, lines for permits to stand in lines that led nowhere, only to other lines. All of them moved very slowly when they moved at all. But this was like no line Rurrik had ever seen. These people were happy. The young Russian began to doubt that it was a line at all. Despite the rain, it seemed to be a street party. Bottles and cigarettes were being passed while people talked, laughed, and even danced. Still, party or no, it would take hours to sort and process this unorthodox mob. Fats would be long gone before the three street buskers got anywhere near the door.

Gizmo broke through the Russian's despair, taking him by the arm and guiding him into the alley that ran next to the building. In the back of Tambura Hall, a long white Cadillac was parked. The front license plate read "Fats". A large black man in evening wear stood guard at the back entrance to the Hall. Rurrik could feel as well as hear the beat of the music through the metal door.

"Sounds like Fats is rolling out the heavy artillery," Gizmo addressed the sentry.

"Gizmo and the Prince, this is a treat," the guard said with genuine delight.

"Rurrik, I want you to meet a friend of mine," Gizmo said, "Rurrik Zimas, this is Muscadine Bolivar."

Muscadine was shadow boxing with Prince Albert but broke off to shake the young Russian's hand. "Pleased to meet you." Rurrik's hand disappeared in the large black paw.

"Muscadine was a boxer. Ranked number three in the world at one time if I remember correctly," Gizmo explained. "Rurrik is in the Russian Navy, at least for now."

"Merchant Marines," Rurrik corrected.

"How are you liking your stay here in New Orleans?" Muscadine asked

"I like it very much. I like American Rock & Roll," Rurrik answered.

"Well don't be standin' out here jawin'. Fats is rocking the hall tonight." Muscadine opened the door and stepped aside. "The fat man will be happy to see you two street musicians and you as well, Mr. Zimas."

Inside the building, the music grew louder and seemed to carry Rurrik along. They made their way down a passageway, and into the wings of the stage. Fats Domino, dressed in a red sequined dinner jacket, sat at the piano. Diamonds flashed as

97

his fingers tumbled over the keys. The building was warm and Rurrik felt uncomfortable in his wrinkled greatcoat. He took the coat off and folded it over his arm.

Gizmo pointed to the stage. "There's your hero. That's Fats at the piano, of course. Joe Harris is on alto sax and over there is Herbert Hardesty and Lee Allen on ...."

"Yes," Rurrik interrupted without taking his eyes from the stage. "And is Ernest McLean, Frank Fields, and Dave Bartholomew with trumpet."

"Perhaps you should be teachin' me about Rock & Roll," Gizmo conceded.

"I have read many of magazines. But I do not know man playing drums."

A small slight man with slick black hair and pencil-thin mustache sat behind the kit.

"That one's by me," Gizmo replied. "Do you know him, Albert?" Prince Albert shook his head and held his hands out to his sides, palms up. "If me and the Prince don't know him he must be new to the Crescent City," Gizmo observed.

Prince Albert tugged at Gizmo's sleeve and then rocked back and forth like he was on a swing.

"You're right, Albert," Gizmo said "He swings it. It's almost as if he must have played in a big band at one time."

Rurrik was hypnotized by the music. "Mr. Gizmo, Mr. Prince, I cannot thank you so much. This is finest day of all my life."

Halfway through the next number, *I'm in Love Again*; Fats noticed Prince Albert dancing in the wings and waved him out to join the band. The Prince dashed to center stage, dropped to his knees, and slid to a stop just short of the edge. The crowd, most of whom knew the Prince from the Quarter, responded with applauds.

Prince Albert sprang to his feet in time to the music and backed up with a series of bounces, his arms out, palms toward the audience. The young boy danced through the rest of the song and through the next number as well. Both the crowd and musicians loved it. At the start of *I'm Walking*, Domino's final number, Prince Albert reached into the wings and pulled Rurrik onto the stage.

The Russian looked out at the hundreds of multicolored faces and froze. The soggy greatcoat fell from his grip. The Prince spun Rurrik away from the audience and clapped his hands to get the Russian's attention. Prince Albert pointed down at his feet and began to dance. Rurrik fell in step. The two did a strutting walk in time to the music. Albert executed his best steps and Rurrik followed like a white shadow.

The crowd was on its feet now and Rurrik took the lead with the Prince hot on his trail. For a finale, Prince Albert broke away, did a handspring that landed him in a split at center stage. Rurrik followed suit flipping over Prince Albert and landing on one knee in front of the younger performer. The Prince bounced up, leapt over Rurrik and came to light, seated on the Russian's knee. The crowd went crazy as Fats bowed and the curtain drew closed.

Roadies scurried onto the stage and began to pack instruments, dismantle amps and roll up electrical cords. Rurrik plucked his greatcoat from the top of a trash can being wheeled away by a member of the clean-up crew.

Fats invited the three street players back to his dressing room for a beer. "Who's the new member of the troupe?" the fat man asked as Muscadine took long-neck bottles of Dixie beer out of a small tombstone-shaped refrigerator and passed them around. He found some RC Cola in the back and handed a bottle to Gizmo and another to Prince Albert.

"This is Rurrik Zimas, late of the Russian Navy," Gizmo announced.

"It is honor to meet you Mr. Domino, you are a true hero of Rock & Roll," Rurrik stammered.

"Hero? Not me. I got Rose Marie and the kids to think about. I can't afford to be a hero. But I'm glad you got to see my farewell performance."

"What are you talking about, farewell?" Gizmo asked

The big man took a long pull on his beer. "Farewell. You heard it right. I'm going to cut some sides for that big project Sam Phillips is working on in Memphis and then I'm back to playing the Blues. Rock & Roll just ain't a safe business to be in right now."

"Safe it is," Gizmo countered. "Profitable is what it ain't."

There was a knock on the dressing room door and Muscadine opened it a crack and looked out. "It's Joey," he announced.

"Have him come in," Fats said.

Muscadine opened the door. "This is Joey Cicero," he said by way of introduction as the band's new drummer entered the room. "Joey, this is Rurrik Zimas, Prince Albert, and Gizmo Broussard."

"Gizmo Broussard! I've heard you play" Joey shook hands with the older man. "You were with Fats last time he played Chicago. You had the licks that night."

"Thank you," Gizmo replied. "You're not half bad yourself. Did you play big band up there in Chi-town?"

Joey's demeanor changed markedly. "Me, I played all around," he said dismissively.

"I never thought about it but now that you mention it I can hear the swing band influence in your work," Fats said.

"I've done a little bit of everything."

"Have a beer?" Muscadine offered.

"No thanks," Joey said. "I just wanted to see what time the session is up in Memphis."

"Don't worry about the time," Fats said. "You fly up with us on the plane."

"Well, about the plane ride. You see, I was thinking I would drive up," Joey countered. "I got a sister in Jackson I ain't seen in years."

"I've been hearing about this Memphis project," Gizmo said. "What's the story up there?"

"Phillips is bringing the biggest names in the business into Sun to record. He's planning the greatest Rock & Roll album ever made. Double album, maybe three if he gets enough stuff," Fats explained.

"He'll get enough if what I been hearin' is true," Muscadine stated. "They say Elvis nailed his cuts. Did his best work right before going into the army. And the others have been there, Chuck Berry, Jerry Lee...."

"And that's just what I been talkin' about," Fats interrupted. "Elvis, Berry, Jerry Lee, Carl Perkins. One by one they record for Sun and one by one they get taken out of the line-up. They get arrested or drafted or wreck their cars. The method is always different, but the end result is always the same. One more set and then I'm out of the Rock & Roll business."

Rurrik thought about it. Fats was right. Tragedy seemed to befall Rock & Roll stars at an alarming rate.

"You really quitting?" Joey Cicero asked.

"Johnny Cash went back to playing country music and as far as I can see they left him alone. I'm cutting my sides and then I'm taking myself out of the game before somebody does it for me. I'm going back home to Mother Blues. There is something going on out there and that something don't like Rock & Roll music."

"The days of Rock & Roll are numbered. It's a fad. The Blues will always be with us," Joey said. "Say, I just might take you up on that offer to fly to Memphis. I can always visit my sister on the way back. I'll have more time to spend with her that way."

"Plane leaves Friday morning, eight sharp. We don't wait for nobody," Muscadine cautioned as he opened the door and let Joey out.

"Are you really giving up Rock & Roll or is this just a ploy to get a bigger percentage of the gate here at the hall?" Gizmo asked.

"I'm as serious as Bishop Sheen," Fats replied.

"But Mr. Domino, you are one of greatest. You cannot quit," Rurrik protested.

"Your friend Gizmo here is one of the best sidemen ever lived," Muscadine pointed out. "Could have made the big time but gave it up because he was afraid of flying. Different fears for different folks."

Rurrik looked at Gizmo. "It just don't feel right, being up in the air like that," Gizmo explained.

Fats had finished changing now. "We did that gig in Chicago, the one Joey talked about, the one where Gizmo played with me. I flew the whole band up there. It was a smooth flight, not so much as a hiccup. Still, we had to send Gizmo all the way back down to the Big Easy by bus."

They had left the dressing room and were crossing the stage.

"I don't travel well in the air," Gizmo said. "I'm not very aerodynamic."

"He don't travel well by bus either," Muscadine countered. "We didn't see his sorry ass again for nearly six months."

"Well, I ran into friends in Saint Looie and, I'll be the first to admit, I had more than a little problem with the booze back then," Gizmo said. "Flyin' just ain't safe. You heard what happened to Penniman didn't you?"

"Penniman? He's over in Europe somewhere." Fats said.

"Richard Penniman, Little Richard Penniman?" Rurrik asked with disbelief.

"His plane caught fire and had to make an emergency landing is all," Gizmo stated. "When Little Richard got off that plane he was all shook up. They say he found Jesus up there in the sky and has given up Rock and Roll."

Fats grabbed Gizmo by the arm and spun him around. "You know he recorded for Phillips right before he left? Look Gizmo,

I'm tellin' you there's something going on here. First Elvis, then Berry, then Perkins, then the Killer, and now you tell me Little Richard almost cashed in."

"Don't you think you might be trying to build something out of what ain't nothing but a series of coincidences?" Gizmo said. "Elvis just had his number come up in the draft is all. Chuck Berry always did like the women, gettin' caught with an underage one wasn't such a big surprise. Jerry Lee is crazy, always has been. He'll marry his dog next. And Perkins was in a car wreck, Fats. A car wreck happens every two minutes out there. In some respects, they're worse than planes."

The fat man let go of Gizmo's arm. "It started when they drafted Elvis. One by one they are taking the big names in Rock & Roll off the board."

The group left the theater by the rear exit. Outside, the rain had stopped but the mist hung heavy. Rurrik, once again, donned his coat.

"Who is this 'they' you're referring to and why would 'they' want to stop rock music?" Gizmo asked.

Muscadine pointed out two figures in a dark doorway down the alley and across the street. "You might start by asking that pair over there. I'm betting they ain't with the Russian Navy."

Rurrik swiveled and saw the two men, one tall, one short and squat. They were both wearing heavy coats and wide-brimmed hats which made them unrecognizable. The shadowy figures left the doorway and slipped down the sidewalk and out of sight.

Muscadine slid behind the wheel of the Cadillac and Fats got into the passenger's seat.

"Look Gizmo, I'm going up to Memphis day after tomorrow to make those cuts for Sun. Why don't you come along? This is going to be the greatest Rock & Roll collection ever. I'm one of the last ones on the list, me and Holly. I'll need the best I can get playing behind me and there is always room for you. This is a paying gig. Meet me at the airport, fly up with us? I'll talk to the pilot, maybe you can sit up front with him."

"Don't hold the plane, Fats?" Gizmo countered.

Fats laughed. "I'm serious now, call me tomorrow if you think you can make it." He reached out the window and shook hands with Prince Albert passing the young man folding money in the process. Next, he shook hands with Rurrik. "Nice meeting you, Rurrik. You should try and get Gizmo to bring you up to Memphis with him. New Orleans is a Jazz and Blues town but, now-a-days, Memphis is all about Rock & Roll."

CHAPTER 9

When the Cadillac had gone, the three street musicians crossed the alley and sat on a loading dock. "I'll bet that's gonna be some session up there in Memphis," Gizmo looked in the direction of the departed car.

Prince Albert jumped to his feet and flapping his arms soared up and down the alley. "Oh no," Gizmo protested. "You can just forget about that. I ain't flying in no airplane. Not even to play back-up to Gabriel and his horn."

Albert hunkered down and glided around the alley as if steering an imaginary automobile. "Now there are a lot of problems with that idea aren't there?" Gizmo chided. "Number one, we ain't got no car."

The Prince blew the make-believe horn and pointed at Gizmo and then made kissing sounds. "Yeah, OK, I have a car over at Maureen's. But neither Maureen nor that old DeSoto has gotten much attention of late. Not much chance of getting the car started and all the way to Memphis and, at this point, Maureen is likely to peel my hide if I so much as go near it."

Prince Albert pointed at Rurrik and then did an exaggerated sailor's dance. "Yeah, right, we could take a boat or stow away on a river barge and maybe get to Memphis by springtime," Gizmo said.

The Prince pushed Rurrik forward. "I know a little of cars, Russian cars. I could go to look," Rurrik offered.

"Well, even if we got the car running it's nearly five hundred miles to Memphis. How we gonna get money for food and gas? The only way we got of making a living is that guitar and ain't no living way Maxie is gonna let us take it off of the steps of Federal Pawn let alone all the way to Memphis."

Rurrik looked down at his greatcoat and then at Gizmo and Prince Albert. "Mr. Maxie was much interested in my coat. Perhaps we will trade guitar for coat."

Prince Albert shook his head from side to side and brushed invisible lint from Rurrik's coat. He combined the bills Fats Domino had given him along with his share of the day's take and held the money out. Rurrik held out the money he had as well.

Gizmo played his last ace. "You two got it all figured out, don't you? Well, tell me this; Maureen has got that car parked slap up against her house, just how are we going to get it without her knowing?"

Prince Albert jumped up onto the loading dock and pretended to knock at an invisible door. He stepped back and did a deep bow as the unseen door opened.

"You got to be kidding me," Gizmo said. "Maureen's birthday was last month, and I clean forgot it. She's a lot more likely to take a fry pan and knock me a windin' than she is to let me near that car."

Prince Albert knocked again at the door, this time he held one hand behind his back. When the invisible door opened, he pulled out his hand to reveal a make-believe bouquet of flowers which he sniffed and presented. For a finale to his little pantomime Albert held his hands over his heart and pumped them in an exaggerated beat while he smiled in mock ecstasy and rolled his eyes upward.

"All right, all right," Gizmo relented. "The two of you have wore me down. I sure would love to play with Fats in Memphis. It can't hurt to walk over to Maureen's and do a little reconnaissance."

On St. Louis Street the three passed a graveyard populated with marble mausoleums and live oaks draped with Spanish moss. The cemetery was surrounded by a high stone wall and the iron entrance gate was closed and locked. Prince Albert crossed himself, scurried over the gate, and disappeared into the darkness.

Rurrik and Gizmo walked to the end of the block, leaned against the cemetery wall, and waited. Across the street was an imposing building of dark stone. A stylized carving of a sunrise spanned the lintel above the front entrance.

"That's the Orleans Parish Prison," Gizmo explained. "It faces due east and when the summer sun comes up it gets hotter than Hades in there. That fact, and the decoration above the door, is why people around here call it the House of the Rising Sun. There's an old folk song was written about it."

For some reason the thought of all those prisoners in there, in the summer, sweltering caused Rurrik to shudder. He pulled his greatcoat tight around his thin body.

In a few minutes, they heard a low whistle from behind the wall at their back. A large bouquet of fresh flowers flew over the barrier followed by the Prince. "Fresh flowers are hard to find this time of year," Gizmo said as he and Rurrik joined Prince Albert. "One nice thing about New Orleans, they have a deep respect for the dead."

When they reached Maureen's, Gizmo tip-toed up the steps to the porch and spied in through the glass beside the door. Maureen, a handsome woman, was sleeping in a comfortable chair in front of the radio. "She looks like she's settled in for the night. Maybe we should come back in the morning."

Gizmo turned to leave but Prince Albert thrust the flowers into the older man's hands and pushed him back toward the door. "Don't you think that two corpses in the same night is quite a bit to ask from one bunch of flowers," the old musician turned once again to leave.

The Prince ducked under Gizmo's arm and rang the doorbell. Gizmo spun, flailing at Albert with the flowers. The Prince vaulted over the railing, a little too quickly for Gizmo's thrust. The bouquet caught only the porch post sending flower petals spraying into the air.

Maureen peered out through the side light and, recognizing Gizmo, threw the door open. Gizmo spun to face Maureen and hurriedly stuck the remains of the bouquet behind his back. "You certainly have your nerve coming around here," the woman said.

Gizmo sputtered for words and then thrust the battered bouquet out toward the angry woman. She slapped the remaining stems and broken blooms out of his hand.

"If this is a bad time for you, I could just come back later," Gizmo pulled his collar up around his ears, ducked and turned to go.

"Oh, no, you don't," Maurine grabbed him by the shoulders. She spun Gizmo around yet again and pushed him into the house with force, kicking the door closed behind her with her foot.

Rurrik and Prince Albert could not make out what was being said behind the closed door, but it was clear that Maureen was doing all the talking. In a few minutes, the door opened, and Gizmo came back out. He bent to retrieve the flowers while Maureen kept a firm grip on the back of his collar. When he had the flowers in hand, she pulled him back through the door and slammed it shut again.

Rurrik and Albert sat on the steps and waited. After a while, the door opened again and this time it was Maureen alone. She handed a stack of blankets and pillows to Rurrik along with a set of car keys. "I believe there are some tools in the trunk if you boys need them, and you might find a flashlight in the glove compartment."

The old DeSoto was, as Gizmo had predicted, parked next to the house. Rurrik found the tools and several quarts of oil in the spacious trunk. The flashlight in the glove box was dead but the streetlight next to the house gave out a good deal of light. In Russia, a driver must remove the side mirrors from his car when parking it for any length of time. If the driver did not, somebody else would. The young Russian deftly removed one of the mirrors and gave it to the Prince who positioned it to reflect the light from the street lamp into the engine compartment.

The former Russian auto mechanic and cab driver was not surprised at how much he recognized in the American car. He traced the plug wires to the distributor and looked in at the points. They were badly burnt and pitted. He found a piece of sandpaper in the toolbox and set about filing the contacts smooth. Next, he removed the spark plugs, cleaned them, and re-gapped them using his thumbnail as a gauge. He replaced the plugs and pinched the wires tightly back in place.

Rurrik removed the air cleaner, beat the worst of the dirt out of it, and set it aside. He blew out the fuel line and pulled the top off the carburetor to clean the float chamber. The brake fluid level was high, and the fluid seemed to be clear. Rurrik pulled the dip stick and found the oil to be dirty and low by a quart and a half. He retrieved oil from the trunk and filled the engine precisely.

"We will try it now."

Prince Albert stepped back and covered his ears while Rurrik turned the key. Nothing happened; the battery was dead. The Prince looked in at the battery, nodded his head, picked up a pair of pliers and disappeared into the dark alley behind the house.

Rurrik took the plugs out of the battery and ran his pinky down the holes to check the water level. Several of the cells were low. He found a soda bottle under the seat, filled it with water from the hose in a neighboring yard and carefully poured it into the dry cells. Next, he looked at the tires. They were short on tread, but the sidewalls were not badly checked, and they sounded good when he thumped them with his finger. The radiator was full and there was well over half a tank of gas.

He was just finishing up when Prince Albert returned laboring under the weight of a battery that was roughly the same size and shape as the one in the old DeSoto. Rurrik made sure the plugs were tight on the borrowed battery and then motioned for Prince Albert to get in behind the wheel of the DeSoto. When the Prince was ready, Rurrik turned the borrowed battery upside down and, making sure the terminals were lined up, set it down on top of the battery in the DeSoto. Balancing the loaner in place with one hand he held his free hand out to the side where Prince Albert could see it and spun his index finger. A finger spun in such a manner is the universal signal for the man behind the wheel to try the key and Prince Albert did.

The engine turned over but did not start. Rurrik spun his finger once again and then cupped his hand and placed it over the carburetor. The engine turned twice more, caught, coughed, backfired loudly, died, and caught again. Thick, blue-black smoke poured from the tailpipe. Rurrik spread his fingers above the carburetor to let in more air. The smoke subsided considerably and changed in color from the black of unburned fuel to the blue of burning oil. He waited until the engine began to smooth out and then removed his hand from the carburetor, lowered the battery to the ground and replaced the air filter.

While the Prince returned the battery Rurrik checked over the engine one last time. The heater valve was stuck, and he forced it open with a pair of pliers. When the interior of the car was warm and the engine had run long enough to recharge the battery, Rurrik shut off the ignition. The two mechanics divided up the blankets and pillows and bedded down for the night.

Just past dawn, they were quietly roused by Gizmo. "Is she running?"

By way of answer, Rurrik slid the key into the ignition and was about to turn it when Gizmo reached over and grabbed his hand, "This old DeSoto is prone to backfire from time to time. Why don't we push her a block or so and try again?"

After a block or two of pushing the car, Rurrik got in and started the engine once again. He readied himself for the backfire and the Prince put his fingers in his ears but it didn't happen.

"I'd like to believe this car is cured of that little problem, but I know better," Gizmo said.

They drove to Gizmo and Prince Albert's modest apartment, had a quick breakfast, and gathered some items for the road. Gizmo held up one of his shirts in front of Rurrik. "Way too big in the chest and the sleeves are about an inch and a half short. One or the other would be bad but I believe the two should even each other out."

"Do you think I should go to the Federal Building and defect before we leave?" Rurrik asked.

"No telling how long a genuine defection could take. We might better wait till we get back from Memphis."

When Maxie arrived at Federal Pawn at nine, the three buskers were waiting. The old pawnbroker put up token resistance, but he knew the value of having one of the best street acts working on his front doorsteps. Maxie even threw in a phone call for Gizmo to call Memphis Recording and leave a message for Fats telling him that they would join him. By ten the pilgrims were passing through Kenner and turning north on Highway 61.

CHAPTER 10

Gizmo drove slowly while Rurrik sat in the front seat trying to locate chords on the guitar. Prince Albert rode in the back, drumming on the leather upholstery as he danced in his seat. Outside the car window, there was plenty for the young Russian to look at. Fields of cotton, fields of cane, pine woods and swamps of tupelo and cypress filled the distance between the small towns. Here and there were moss-covered graveyards with their marble angels and stone war heroes.

Occasionally a fine plantation house could be seen at the end of an alley of moss-laden live oaks. At times the road seemed to be passing through a tunnel formed by spreading pecan trees on both sides of the road. Here and there, beneath the trees and along the edges of the fields were rows of tar-paper shacks. On the front porch of many of the shacks were washing machines or refrigerators or both. Almost every house, even the most decrepit, had at least one car. Rurrik marveled at the wealth. In America, even the poor were rich by Russian standards.

A few of the large plantation houses were empty. Some of the shacks and a number of the commercial buildings in the small towns were vacant as well. In Moscow, Rurrik had never seen empty buildings unless they were rendered unsafe by crumbling concrete. Some of the abandoned shacks looked to be beyond repair but most of the vacant plantation houses and commercial buildings in the towns appeared to be solid structures. It was a rich country indeed that could leave buildings unoccupied.

After a while, Gizmo pulled over onto the shoulder. Rurrik checked the engine and added half a quart of oil and then made some minor adjustments to the carburetor. "Your turn to drive," Gizmo said. The Russian had driven a taxi around the streets of Moscow but there was quite a difference between a Zis and this American car with its powerful engine. Rurrik was grateful for the straight road. It took some time for him to get used to the responsive gas pedal and loose steering but there was little traffic and soon he had the old machine up to cruising speed. By the time they reached Baton Rouge he was piloting the car like he was born to it. About forty miles north of the state capital, they passed a sign which welcomed the trio to the Great State of Mississippi. Rurrik looked around for guards and a guardhouse.

"Do we not have to stop for customs?" Rurrik asked.

"I believe they do that kind of thing in California, but I don't see the state of Mississippi puttin' out the effort," Gizmo said

"What about Prince Albert?" Rurrik said. "I worry because of Mr. Chuck Berry being arrested for crossing state line with a child in his car."

"From what I hear, that was a completely different set of circumstances. Besides, don't nobody care what happens to the Prince." Gizmo said.

Prince Albert leaned forward and drummed on Gizmo's shoulders while pointing to the back of the older man's head. Gizmo laughed. "Well, maybe I care, but just a little."

The three stopped in Woodville for lunch. Gizmo and Rurrik went into a cafe on the town square and ordered food. The four men playing bourre at a folding card table looked with suspicion at the pale Russian and the old musician. The two travelers made their order to go. A few miles north of town they pulled over beside the Buffalo River and ate. "It would be better if Elvis was from Soviet Union," Rurrik observed between spoon of red beans and rice.

"Better for who?" Gizmo questioned

"Elvis was only child, right? No brother, no sister," Rurrik reasoned. "In Russia we do not take the only child into the army unless we are in war. I am only child. I know such things."

"We don't here either," Gizmo countered "At least not as a rule."

"Who can break such rule?" Rurrik asked.

"Well, the federal government would be the only one who could do that," Gizmo said and then caught himself. "Now holt on one second. You're turnin' into as big a paranoid as Fats."

"What is paranoid?"

"Somebody who sees a sinister plot behind every little traffic accident and airplane engine fire."

Just north of Vicksburg they stopped for gas at a white, streamlined gas station. Rurrik and Gizmo used the restroom in the back of the station while Prince Albert went to the outhouse marked Colored. Behind the station, the land dropped off steeply. Level fields of rich, dark earth stretched to the horizon. The uniformed attendant wiped the windshield and checked the oil.

"You're down half a quart and this needs to be changed," the attendant said.

"Put in the half quart and give us the rest in the can if you would?" Gizmo said. "We plan to have it changed in Memphis."

When Rurrik paid for the gas and oil the attendant handed him a cardboard box containing a Melmac serving dish. "We only have money for gas," Rurrik explained and tried to hand the dish back to the young man in the uniform.

The attendant refused the box. "Free with five gallons or more."

Rurrik looked over at Gizmo. Gizmo nodded and Rurrik handed the box to Prince Albert in the back seat. "This is wonderful country," Rurrik observed.

"It's pretty damn good as far as countries go but if it were truly wonderful then the Prince could use whatever bathroom he wanted to use."

Rurrik turned the ignition key and the DeSoto shot a ball of fire from the tailpipe. It singed the white pant leg of the attendant who was crossing behind the car.

In a short while, the road dropped down to the plain that Rurrik had seen from the station. The land here was much different than any he had seen on the journey so far. Gone were the pine trees and sandy soil. The gently rolling fields of limited size had now given way to vast, and almost perfectly flat expanses. Cotton stubble stretched to the distant tree line in every direction. Even in this dormant season, Rurrik could sense the fertility in the soil. The thin blue sky, like faded denim, made the landscape appear to be even larger than it was. To the northwest, wispy, yellow-white clouds were building.

The highway passed through Onward and on into Rolling Fork. "What do your magazines tell you about this town?" Gizmo asked.

"I do not know Rolling Fork."

"Home of Muddy Waters, father of the Chicago Blues."

They bumped over the railroad tracks in the middle of the town.

"The magazines say Blues was major influence on Rock & Roll," Rurrik stated.

Gizmo pointed out the corner where Muddy used to busk. "Major influence on us all. And yet little is known about the land it grew out of or the pioneers of the genre. Take Muddy for instance. His real name was, according to sources, McKinley, McKinley Morganfield. Some say that wasn't his real name and he wasn't from Rolling Fork at all but from someplace over in Issaquena County. Mystery surrounds most of the other early Blues men as well. They seemed to have risen up like ghosts from the black Delta soil."

Rurrik learned to anticipate the towns by spotting the community's water tower, cotton gin or grain dryer on the horizon. The wind blew steadily from the northwest, the direction of the clouds, and he had to hold the steering wheel cocked at ten degrees to compensate. It began to feel as if he was once again at sea and the sea reminded him of his mission. "I must remember to defect just as soon as we get back to New Orleans," he said to Gizmo by way of reminder.

"No problem," Gizmo assured. "Look, if you're worried about it, I'm sure they got a Federal Building in Memphis. Not too many disappointed ideologues make it that far the upriver. Likely you won't have to wait in line or nothing."

"Can I defect at any Federal Building?" Rurrik asked.

"Sure, why not," Gizmo said with uncertain certainty. "And if they don't want you, why, we can just run you by the post office."

At Hollandale, they turned east on Route 12 and pulled over to the shoulder of the road. Rurrik added another half quart of oil and Gizmo took over behind the wheel. The wind was now more to their back causing the car to pick up speed. Gizmo turned north once again at Belzoni. A few miles past Morgan City he pulled the car to a stop in a weedy gravel parking lot beside the old Quito Zion Church.

The church, framed of yellow pine and built on low brick piers, had little to recommend it, The piers had settled unevenly, skewing windows, bowing siding, sagging the roof line, and spreading the shingles. The church was white although the most recent paint job appeared to be about ten years old. It looked to Rurrik as if the painter had only a short ladder and couldn't reach the top four rows of siding. Most of the steeple in front, squat as it was, could not be reached by the brush at all. The result was a two-tone effect of pealing white paint below and almost paint-free gray boards above.

Gizmo brought the car to a stop at the far end of the gravel parking lot. "There's somebody here you have to visit if you want to learn about Rock & Roll."

Rurrik and Prince Albert followed the old musician around behind the church, through a broken gate, and into a crude cemetery. The switchgrass filled in high between the rows of simple wooden crosses, mossy concrete markers, and the occasional small headstone. The wind was not blowing strongly but it was constant. The dry grass rustled like a soft, unending, drum roll. Here and there Rurrik could see glass jars and faded artificial flowers tangled in the weeds. Near the back of the graveyard, Gizmo stopped at a small unadorned stone. The neck of a broken bottle lay upon the marker along with cigarettes and a guitar pick.

"They say Robert Johnson is buried here," Gizmo explained. "I doubt they ever heard much about him in Russia. Hell, outside of this part of Mississippi he ain't known very much anywhere. They call him 'King of the Delta Blues' but he didn't start out that way. He was just a kid, a Bluesman wannabe who would get up on stage and play when the regular band was on break. Then he disappeared over across the river in Arkansas for six or eight months. When he came back, he was more than just a good Bluesman, he was the best. The story goes; he went down to the crossroads one moonless night and made a deal with the Devil. He traded his soul for the gift. Like I said, he was the greatest of the Blues singers, but it was only a few short years before the song ended for Robert. Now he's just one more Delta ghost."

Rurrik looked down at the slight depression in the earth in front of the stone. "I have read about Blues, but I am not sure what is."

"The Blues is a music born of melancholy sadness that penetrates all the way to a man's soul," Gizmo explained.

124

Rurrik looked down at his feet. "I don't mean s-o-l-e, the bottom of your foot, I mean s-o-u-l, the divine principle in man, his spiritual essence, the mortal core of his being," Gizmo stated as he thumped on Rurrik's chest.

"I have heard people sing Blues to make themselves feel better."

"That, or to make everybody around you feel just as bad as you do, which amounts to the same thing."

"I believe I have had the Blues."

"The Blues in Russia?" Gizmo looked at him with skepticism. "More likely you were just clinically depressed. The Blues is, more or less, an American thing. I'm not sure you can have the Blues in Russia. I know you can't have them in France or Denmark or any place like that. You ever been in jail?"

"Yes, several times. Twice I was in the prison for listening to Rock & Roll music."

"Good heavens. No wonder you're paranoid about this Rock & Roll conspiracy. They put you in jail in Russia for playing music. Maybe you have had the Blues after all... anyway, this is Robert Johnson's grave and it don't mean much to most but it does to me, and it might to you."

Rurrik looked at the clouds on the northwest horizon. The wind had gained in velocity, and he had to speak somewhat louder. "I have never heard his music."

"Me neither," Gizmo said. "There's few people who have heard him play. They say he made a recording down in Texas, but I haven't heard that either. He died back in the 30's. Some say he was chasen' skirts and got poisoned by a jealous husband, some say the Devil came to collect on the debt. But I don't see any reason you and Domino have to accept either story. Could be J. Edgar Hoover had him killed. As soon as we get done in Memphis, I think you and the fat man should come right back down here with shovels and start digging into this conspiracy.

Out of respect, Rurrik bent to remove the bottleneck from the grave marker, but Gizmo stopped him. "That was put there on purpose. A tribute to Robert. A good Bluesman can make you weep by playing slide guitar with a bottleneck on his finger."

The three looked up to see a large black sedan roll slowly past the church. It took them by surprise. The steady sound of the wind in the grass had kept them from hearing its approach. The black car slowed, stopped, and then turned around. The wind stopped as well.

Gizmo grabbed the Prince by the arm and began to walk quickly out of the graveyard. Rurrik fell in behind. With the wind in retreat, they could hear the black sedan crunch gravel as it parked out of sight on the far side of the church. Gizmo began to run.

The old musician reached the driver's side and slid in behind the wheel. The black sedan was parked about twenty yards away, but occupant, or occupants, could not be clearly seen. Rurrik banged his head as he tumbled in on the passenger's side. Prince Albert dove through the open window into the back seat.

Gizmo fumbled trying to get the keys in the ignition and dropped them down by his feet. He bent double and swept the dirt-covered floor mat with his hands. Rurrik bent to help, and in the confusion, the keys were knocked down through a hole in the rusted quarter panel and out onto the ground.

CHAPTER 11

"Can I help you, gentlemen?" The words came from outside the car.

Rurrik and Gizmo, looking up from the floor, were confronted by the smiling face of an old black man who was standing by the side of the DeSoto. "I saw the car here and just thought I would come back and check," the old black man scooped the keys up with the end of his cane and handed them to Gizmo. "I was the preacher here for many years."

"We just came to visit Robert's grave," Gizmo explained as he nodded his thanks for the retrieved keys.

The old man looked in the direction of the untended graveyard. "Not many come by anymore."

Gizmo followed his gaze. "They'll be back. Anybody looking for the story of the Blues will come lookin' for Robert."

The preacher shook his head sadly. "People don't care much for the Blues nowadays. The Russians put up that Sputnik and now everybody is into the future. Don't nobody care for the past no more."

"Blues turned into Rhythm & Blues and Rhythm & Blues grew into Rock & Roll and, despite what my young Russian friend here might think, Rock & Roll will never die. Every generation will go looking for their roots and every generation will find their way here." Gizmo said.

"I'm sorry," the old black man said to Rurrik. "I didn't know you was a Russian. I like Sputnik myself. My wife and I used to go out in the yard on a winter's night and watch it go by."

"Thank you," Rurrik said. "I am enjoying very much my visit to United States."

"You must have been misinformed," the old preacher said as he turned away. "This ain't the United States, this here is the Delta."

When the old man had gone, Gizmo turned to his two companions. "What was you two runnin' for? Wasn't nothing but an old preacher man."

Prince Albert bounced up and down in the back seat and poked his finger at Gizmo. "OK, maybe I ran too," Gizmo conceded.

"You were first to run," Rurrik said.

The three left the parking area of the church and drove north toward Greenwood. Just south of Itta Bena they had to stop as a railroad crossing gate came down barring the road. For a while, Rurrik was content to watch the box cars rolling by from the east and then he noticed the birds. There were hundreds of them, and they passed by overhead in an endless stream. Small black birds, not hundreds but thousands, and coming from the northwest with the wind at their tail. The wispy, yellow clouds on the horizon, now more clearly defined, had taken on a greenish aura. The wind was back. Even above the rumbling of the train and the whistle of the wind, Rurrik could hear the birds as they called out, urging each other on.

Gizmo called the young Russian's attention back to the train. "This is the Yazoo & Mississippi Valley rail line. Folks around here call it the Yellow Dog."

"Why do they call this the Delta?" Rurrik asked.

"Because it is. All this land you're lookin' at was laid in here millions of years ago by the Mississippi River. They say the topsoil goes down half a mile or more in places. It's just about the richest farmland in the country and just about the poorest people live on it."

"In my country, we say sometimes misfortune can nurture art where riches cannot," Rurrik said.

"Under the Borgia, Italy suffered war, terror, tyranny, and murder and yet they produced Michelangelo, Leonardo, and the Renaissance. Switzerland had five hundred years of law and order, peace and prosperity and what do they have to show for it? - The cuckoo clock," Gizmo mused as the last of the box cars passed.

"That is very much true and very much wise," Rurrik said in admiration.

"I didn't make that up," Gizmo confessed. "Harry Lime said it."

"I do not know Harry Lime," Rurrik admitted

"The Orson Welles character in *The Third Man.* It was a movie. Do you get to see many American movies in Russia?" Gizmo asked.

"We saw *Red River* with Mister John Wayne. They told us Americans are violent, imperialistic people. We saw *The Grapes of Wrath.*"

"Henry Fonda, Jane Darwell, John Carridine, great movie." Gizmo observed.

"The Soviet Government wanted us to see how bad things were in United States," Rurrik explained. "They make movie available for everyone."

"That makes sense. All those proletariat Okies being driven from their homes by the landed bourgeois and the capitalistic bankers."

"Maybe some saw that in movie, but we did not. We all wanted to be like Okies. They had cars."

Rurrik looked at Prince Albert slumped over in the back seat. Even in sleep, the young man tapped his foot in perfect time. "You are good friend to the Prince."

"He has been a good friend to me. About three years ago I quit drinking and started to put my life back together. All I had left of any value was that guitar. One day I was playing on the corner for loose change when Prince Albert came up and just started dancing. Been with me ever since."

"Where is his voice?" Rurrik asked.

"Don't know. He's never said a word to me. Took him to a specialist about a year ago. That's how the guitar got in hock," Gizmo explained. "Nothing physical, he just don't talk."

"Do you know his mother and father?"

"I assume he had one of each at some point, but I wouldn't know where they are. In the pocket of that jacket, he has on is a flat tobacco can, Prince Albert Tobacco. In the can is a wedding photo."

"Could you find them with photo?" Rurrik asked.

"I had a friend who works with the police department check missing persons. No match for the Prince. If his parents are still out there someplace, they aren't looking for him. I was afraid to take it further."

"Do people in this country fear the police?"

"Not the way they do in Russia. You can't go to prison here for playing Rock & Roll, at least not yet, but the organization has its flaws. I could turn the Prince over to the system but, parents or no parents, I'm afraid that would be the last I would see of him. The Prince needs me but I need him just as much. I used to go on the wagon every few years, but it didn't last long. My strong feeling is that we are both better off together than we would be apart."

For a while, Rurrik watched the fields of cotton stubble pass by outside his window. As the car came abreast of each row the young Russian could, for a split second, see down the line and almost to the horizon. The rows flashed hypnotically by and soon Rurrik was also asleep. He had not spent long in the Moscow prison cell, but it was frequently the setting for his dreams. He found himself again in that cell.

When he awoke, the car was stopped near the front of a long line of cars. Men in faded black and white striped pants, denim jackets, and straw hats were working on the shoulder of the road. They had been shoveling dirt from the drainage ditch into wheelbarrows which were, in turn, being pushed up a ramp made of planks and into the back of a depression-era dump truck. The holdup was the fault of the truck. Two of the four rear tires had blown while it was turning around in the road. The men in stripes were attempting to lift the truck by means of levers improvised from fence posts. Two prisoners stood in the back of the truck shoveling dirt back down onto the shoulder to lighten the load. Armed guards in brown uniforms and broad-brimmed hats were supervising the work.

"This gonna take a while," the prisoner who was acting as flagman announced.

"I'd better shut her down and save gas or we won't make it to Memphis," Gizmo said as he switched off the motor.

"Where are we?" Rurrik asked.

134

"We're about five miles from Tutwiler, birthplace of the Blues," Gizmo answered. "Legend has it that the band leader, W.C. Handy, was waiting for a train in Tutwiler when he heard a black field hand singing the Blues. You understand now, Handy didn't know it was the Blues; he just knew it was a new music. W.C. was a showman, and he took it back to Memphis with him and incorporated it into his act."

"Did you ever play Blues?" Rurrik asked.

"Seems like I'm teachin' you far more about the Blues than I am about Rock & Roll. Yes, I've played them, sang them, ate them for dinner, and laid down at night with the Blues for a pillow. There was times I lived the Blues just as surely as these men here."

"Who are they?" Rurrik asked indicating the workers along the side of the road.

"This is a chain gang from Parchman."

"Parchman?"

"Parchman is the state pen, what you might call a gulag. It's about ten miles west of here."

"What did these men do?" Rurrik asked.

"All manner of indiscretion," Gizmo waved his hand inclusively. "Some were robbers or common thieves. Some went as far as murder while others just got on the wrong side of a vindictive county judge."

135

Rurrik looked at the men. A few of them wore leg irons. "Does your government send spies to Parchman?"

"I shouldn't think convicted spies would be sent to a state pen like Parchman. More likely spies would go to a federal lock-up like Leavenworth. Say, don't you have enough intrigue in your life, what with this plot to eradicate Rock & Roll? You're not thinking about becoming a spy, are you?"

Rurrik moved quickly to change the subject. "Will we have enough gas to go to Memphis?"

"Well, let's see," Gizmo began to do math in his head. "We're about twenty miles from Clarksdale, Clarksdale to Memphis another seventy-five or so. We been gettin' about seventeen miles to the gallon what with this head wind. Got about three or four gallons left in the tank. Seventy-five, twenty, seventeen, four gallons...carry five, move the decimal... short answer, no. We can hock the guitar in Clarksdale. Half that town is pawn shops."

Prince Albert, who had been sitting quietly awake in the back seat of the car, grabbed the guitar and jumped out of the car.

"Where you goin' with my guitar? You startin' on a life of crime, are you? You and Rurrik the spy are both gonna end up over in Parchman."

Prince Albert began to strum the guitar loudly. Gizmo got out of the car and chased the youth, but Albert stayed one step ahead. Finally, at the very back of the row of cars Gizmo caught the Prince and recovered the instrument. By this time there were many more vehicles in the line. Some people, out of boredom, had gotten out of their cars and were staring at the two musicians. Sensing a captive audience, Gizmo began to play *CC Rider*, a song about a circuit court judge. He played with a heavy beat in a Rock & Roll tempo and sang the words in his best penitentiary voice. The two worked their way back toward the front of the line of cars. Gizmo played and sang while Prince Albert danced between the cars, holding his jacket pocket open to the other motorists as he passed. The motorists, grateful for the entertainment, kept the coins coming.

Near the front of the line, Gizmo broke into *Midnight Special*. The prisoners on the chain gang began to sing along; some even put down their shovels and joined Prince Albert in the dance.

The convicts managed to replace one of the tires on the truck and began to move the old vehicle gingerly from the center of the road. Gizmo and Albert got back into the DeSoto. As soon as the truck cleared the first lane the flagman waved the cars through, first from one direction and then from the other.

Nearly all the cars were past when the replacement tire on the dump truck blew out. The truck dropped down onto the wheel rims and the tailgate fell open causing a shower of dirt to cover the road. The last car to join the line, a dark sedan, braked to a halt just short of the spill. A man on the passenger's side rolled down the window and cursed the prisoners.

Prince Albert counted the money and tapped out the total on Gizmo's back. They had enough for gas, food, and a room for the night if they wanted it. "Let's spend the night in Clarksdale," Gizmo offered. "I know a rooming house there that will accept blacks, whites, and Russians. There is a meat-an-three just down the block that makes cornbread that is a meal unto its own self."

"Will they have red beans and rice?" Rurrik asked.

CHAPTER 12

The next morning the clouds were gone, and the warm Southern sun quickly took the chill from the air. Rurrik removed the spark plugs one by one and the Prince cleaned them of the black, oily buildup. They bought another five gallons of gas on the way out of Clarksdale. This time Rurrik was given a set of two juice glasses with the station's logo on the side. He put them in the back seat along with the serving dish.

The old car reached Memphis early in the afternoon. Highway 61 became Third Street and the trio turned east on Union Avenue. After a mile or two, Gizmo turned off Union and parked the car on Marshall Street half a block down from Taylor's Cafe.

Rurrik picked up the greatcoat which lay on the seat beside him. He took the worn photo from the pocket and read the caption beneath Elvis and Sam Phillips. "Taylor's Cafe" is what it said. He smoothed out the photo and slid it as neatly as possible into his shirt pocket.

A soft wind was blowing from the south as the three buskers walked back toward the corner. Just past Walker Radiator was Memphis Recording Services. Rurrik moved as if in a trance toward the cafe on the corner, but Gizmo halted his progress and directed him into the recording studio.

"Well, Gizmo Broussard," the woman behind the desk in the reception area said. "I didn't think we would ever see you again this side of the pearly gates."

"Hello, Marion," Gizmo said. "You know, I was standing at death's door on numerous occasions, but I always managed to pull myself back. I just had to live to see you one more time. Is Sam in?"

"He and Fats are next door at Taylor's. You should go on over."

In the cafe, Fats Domino and Muscadine Bolivar sat in a red vinyl, chrome, and Formica booth drinking coffee and working on slabs of Karo nut pie. A white man in a sky blue, western cut shirt sat across from the two large black men. "Gizmo and his entourage," Fats announced. "Pull up a table and join us."

Rurrik and Gizmo shifted a table and chairs over against the booth while Prince Albert sparred with Muscadine. "Gizmo, you know Sam, don't you?" Fats asked.

Gizmo shook hands with the man in the blue shirt. "Sure do."

"Gizmo played for an Orbison session here at Sun back about two or three years ago," Phillips recalled, "One doesn't forget a musician like Gizmo."

"Roy had a voice like an archangel at a rodeo. I was just fortunate to be in the choir," Gizmo mused. "This is my friend from Russia, Rurrik Zimas."

"Pleased to meet you," Sam said.

"I am honored to meet you, Mr. Phillips," Rurrik stated. "Your Sun records are precious in my country."

"Precious, I guess that would be a compliment but, if I was you, I wouldn't tell Jerry Lee that you think his records are precious," Phillips said.

"And this is Prince Albert," Muscadine pointed out. "Just about the finest hoofer there is. If I could move my feet like him, I'd have been champion of the world." Prince Albert performed an exaggerated tap dance while he shadowboxed around the cafe.

The group sat down at the table and the waitress came over. "And what will you recent additions have?" she asked.

"Fill them up Margaret, and charge it to Sun," Sam Phillips announced.

"Very kind of you, Sam," Gizmo said. "I'll have chicken fried steak, creamed gravy, creamed potatoes, nothing green, and an RC."

Albert dropped the boxing routine, turned his index fingers into horns, and pawed the floor like a bull preparing to charge. "The Prince will have a cheeseburger and fries," Gizmo added.

"And what about you?" the waitress asked as she turned to face Rurrik.

The Russian stared at the young woman. His jaw went slack. It was her, the Asian waitress from the photo. His hand went up and covered the pocket that held the photo. It was as if he were afraid she might see it through the fabric of his shirt. To him she was the most beautiful creature he had ever seen. She appeared to be in her late teens. Her shiny black hair was pulled back in a ponytail and her skin was the color of honey. She had high cheekbones and her almond-shaped were as black as her hair. The yellow and white waitress uniform, with Margaret Soo embroidered above the pocket, did not fit her slender body any better than Rurrik's uniform fit his, but it mattered not. Rurrik was thunder-struck. He could not speak but only sat with his hand over his heart.

"Something to eat, maybe a cold drink, hot coffee?" she asked and then looked to Gizmo for help.

"That one talks," Gizmo assured her. "At least he did when we came in here. Go ahead, Rurrik, order. Maybe they have red beans and rice."

"Yes, madam," Rurrik looked at the girl and not the menu. "Do you have the red beans and rice?"

"Oh, I'm sorry," Margaret said with genuine regret. "We do them on Thursday, that's Cajun night."

"I will have the chicken and steak fried also."

"Chicken fried steak," Margaret corrected as she wrote the order on her pad.

"My English is not good," Rurrik admitted. "Please, could you tell me, is that chicken or is that steak?"

"You'll have to forgive the lad," Gizmo interjected. "Rurrik is from Russia, northern Russia; they don't have delicacies like chicken fried steak in that part of the world."

"Are you really a Russian?" the girl asked. "We certainly don't have Russians back in Marigold. I don't believe I've ever met anybody from as far away as that."

"You met Little Richard didn't you, Margaret? He's from outer space," Sam Phillips offered.

"Now there is one scary thought," she said.

"What is?" Fats asked.

"The possibility that there might be a planet out there populated by millions of people just like Little Richard," Margaret explained. "As for the chicken fried steak, it's not chicken, that much is for sure, but I don't think you could call it steak either. We take a marginal cut of beef, beat it all over, both sides, with a waffle-headed hammer, batter it up, fry it in fat and cover it with white gravy that has the texture but not the personality of grade-school craft paste. We put the gravy over

143

on the creamed potatoes as well. You can take your knife and cut a cross-section through the spuds and not be able to tell where the potatoes end and the gravy begins."

"Damn, but don't Margaret make that sound good," Muscadine licked his lips. "I'm sorry I already ate."

"If you're going to be traveling in the South then you'll have to eat one at some time or another. You might as well get it out of the way now while you're still young and relatively healthy. I'll bring you some mixed vegetables with that just to break up the monochrome scheme," Margaret said as she turned from the table.

Prince Albert stepped in front of Margaret as she was leaving and pointed at the mixer behind the counter.

"I believe the Prince would like a milkshake with his burger," Gizmo explained.

"I'm sorry hon, the Multimixer is out of order," Margaret explained. "How about a float?"

Prince Albert grabbed Rurrik by the sleeve, pulled him to his feet, and pushing him toward Margaret, pointed once again at the mixing machine.

"Rurrik is a machinist in the Russian Navy. Why don't you let him have a look at the Multimixer?" Gizmo suggested.

"Do they have Multimixers in Russia?" Margaret asked Gizmo.

144

"Probably not," Gizmo observed. "But he fixed my car and got it running enough to get it up here from New Orleans."

"That is high praise," Fats chimed in, "for I have seen Gizmo's car."

Rurrik was flustered to be so close to Margaret and fumbled for words. "Perhaps I could take a see, I mean, take and look."

"That would be great if you could," Margaret said. "Last time it went down we had to wait two weeks for the repairman and then another two weeks for the parts to be shipped from Chicago."

Rurrik and Prince Albert went behind the counter where the pistachio green mixer sat on a shelf while Margaret placed the order with the cook in the kitchen.

"I believe ole Rurrik has been taken by Margaret," Sam observed.

"If he can fix small appliances anything like he can dance that mixer will be running to New Orleans," Fats said. "He and The Prince put on a show in Tambora Hall that... well, if you could record dance that number would go gold."

Margaret chatted with the cook for a moment and then went over behind the counter where Rurrik and Prince Albert were working on the machine. The Prince was standing on a chair and holding the top of the Multimixer while Rurrik poked around inside with a table knife.

"Are you really in the Russian Navy?" Margaret asked.

145

"I am in Soviet Merchant Marines," Rurrik corrected. "Have you working here long?" Rurrik was hoping to move the conversation onto firmer ground. He did not want to have to lie to Margaret.

"Two years," Margaret said. "I'll bet you've been all over the world."

"Here is problem," Rurrik announced with relief as he pulled the salad plate-sized drive wheel out of the mixer. Wheel is good and shaft is good but key no is good."

"We never needed a key to use it before."

"Key is not like key to door. It is small piece of metal, shape of a moon one half. Holds wheel onto shaft," Rurrik explained.

Margaret put her hands on her hips. "That sounds like another two weeks waiting for this key to come from Chicago."

Prince Albert hung his head and Margaret put her arm around him.

Rurrik placed the wheel back onto the shaft and looked at the key-way. He walked back to the table and removed the hammer and sickle pin from the lapel of his greatcoat which hung on the back of his chair. Bending the cycle part back and forth between his fingers, he returned to the counter. The pot metal pin broke easily. He pressed the sickle part of the pin into the keyway and tapped it down with the handle of the knife. Next, he pushed up on one of the triggers behind the beaters and the machine sprang to life. Both Margaret and the Prince gave

Rurrik a hug. A bit embarrassed by the attention, he picked up one of the stainless-steel cups and the ice cream scoop. "Could you teach me to make milk shake?"

Margaret picked up another of the steel cups and found a second scoop beneath the counter. "Start with the ice cream. You do chocolate, I'll do vanilla. Three scoops."

Rurrik dug into the hard-packed ice cream and came up with half a scoop which he dropped into the cup. Prince Albert tugged at Margaret's sleeve and pointed out Rurrik's shortcoming. "Three full scoops," Margaret advised. "Here at Taylor's, we value our customers." Rurrik set to work and, with a little practice, was able to make up the difference.

"Now we add the milk," Margaret poured from the cardboard carton into both cups. "And next the syrup." She took both cups and held them while Prince Albert worked the syrup pump. "Now the mixer. Are you sure that wheel won't fly out of there and maybe hit somebody right between the eyes?"

Rurrik gave the pin a few more taps and replaced the mixer cover. "In Soviet Union we do not value life highly as you do in USA." The pin held and the shakes came out rich and creamy.

Prince Albert gave the chocolate one to Rurrik and kept the vanilla one himself as the two walked back to the table. The food arrived and the three street performers, whose personal finances had not allowed for breakfast, dug in. "How is it?" Fats asked Rurrik.

"The chicken fried steak is very much good. The potatoes and gravy are very... they are very much Russian," Rurrik said.

"Has Fats been telling you about the conspiracy to destroy Rock & Roll music?" Gizmo asked Sam.

"I have to admit," Sam said "the theory has some validity. It does seem like every artist who recorded here in the past six months has been beset by some form of misfortune, but I don't see why the government would have to resort to subterfuge to try and put me out of business. They just have to keep taxing me the way they have, and I'll be padlocking the doors in another six months."

"You might as well close up shop if your artists keep winding up in jail or in the hospital," Fats said.

"Buddy Holly was in here a few weeks back. He sounded good, by the way, and as far as I know, he's still living," Phillips pointed to a poster on the wall behind the counter. "That is, if you can call a winter bus tour of the frozen tundra living."

Rurrik looked over at the poster. It was a cardboard handbill announcing the Winter Dance Party featuring Buddy Holly, Richie Valens, and the Big Bopper.

"Well, conspiracy or not, we got artists here today. We'll record some this evening and then finish it up tomorrow, if we have to. Pays fifty dollars a day plus expenses," Sam said as he handed Gizmo a wad of folding money. "I've got you gentlemen a room at Ma Atherton's right over on Myrtle Street. It's near the tracks but the traffic on the Southern Line isn't heavy this time of year. Ma is a saint of a woman, and you can walk there from here and back if you need to."

"I'm going to the room to rest up. Why don't you and Prince Albert go down to Lansky Brothers and get some new clothes?" Gizmo handed Rurrik part of the money.

"I do not know Lansky Brothers," Rurrik explained.

"It's down on Beale," Margaret explained as she took off her apron. "I'm off shift until tomorrow. If you give me a ride home, I'll show you Lansky's on the way."

Rurrik looked at the money in his hand. "That is very much kind, but I could not take money."

The old musician waved it off. "Maybe I can't pay my driver, but I can see that he is dressed in proper fashion."

Muscadine joined the conversation. "No offense Rurrik, but those Eastern Bloc threads of yours are in need of an upgrade. That shirt appears to be both too big and too small at the same time. You might consider taking Gizmo up on his offer and it wouldn't hurt to ask Margaret to help you pick out your new ensemble."

"It will be fun," Margaret said as she and Prince Albert hustled Rurrik out of the cafe.

"Come back for the session tonight," Sam offered. "We should start around six."

"Do Merchant Marines get shore leave just like the Navy?" Margaret asked as the three young people drove back down Union Street.

Not only did Rurrik not know the correct answer to the question, but he was also desperate to stay away from that line of inquiry altogether. "Yes, they do," he responded. "Did you say you were from Mongolia?" As soon as he spoke Rurrik realized that in his hurried attempt to change the subject he had asked a truly bonehead question.

"No, I'm from Marigold, not Mongolia. It's a small town in Mississippi," Margaret laughed. "I'm Chinese, well, three-quarters Chinese anyway. The Chinese have been in the Mississippi Delta for generations. They were originally brought here to work the cotton fields, but never took to it. Today nearly every Delta town has a Chinese grocery."

"Do your parents have a grocery?"

"They did but I lost my parents a few years ago. Now I live here in Memphis with my aunt and her husband."

"It is good to have family," Rurrik observed.

"It's a mixed blessing. The Chinese do not value girl children so highly and then there is the problem with my grandfather. He was a Creole from New Orleans. Mixed blood is bad blood to the Chinese."

Late on a winter afternoon was a dormant time for Beale Street. The restaurants were done serving lunch and not quite

150

ready to welcome the dinner crowd. The juke joints and Blues clubs would not even be open for three or four hours. The occasional beer delivery truck was the only sign of the impending storm of music and dance. Despite its quiet winter slumber, Beale was the black Main Street of Memphis and Rurrik could feel the power that lay just below the surface.

Lansky Brothers was where every well-dressed black man and woman in Memphis shopped, but lately it had become a favorite of the ever-growing number of rebellious white youth as well. Jerry Lee Lewis' recording of *Great Balls of Fire* was playing loudly from giant speakers in the four corners of the store as the three entered Lansky's. Prince Albert and Margaret dove in like they were born to shop.

Rurrik stood near the door. His mind was paralyzed, over-stimulated by the rock music and the array of merchandise before him. He could not get his mind around so many racks with so many clothes in so many colors and styles. It was more than he had ever seen before; more than he ever could imagine. He was afraid to leave the relative safety of the door for fear he would not be able to find his way back. The young Russian took a few small steps in the direction Margaret and Albert had headed and then turned to check his position in relationship with the door. When he looked back Margaret and Prince Albert were gone.

Rurrik began to feel lightheaded like he had in the Customs House in New Orleans. He looked around the store but could not bring the kaleidoscope of color and shape into focus. His breath was coming in quick short gulps. He turned and focused his gaze back through the glass door and out into the street. The light gray sidewalk and dark gray street relaxed him somewhat.

"Rurrik, Rurrik," he heard Margaret's voice calling him from a great distance. He turned once again, looked back into the store, and tried to focus.

Margaret took him by the arm. "Are you alright?"

Rurrik was surprised to see her so close.

"Come on. I've found a suit that I think is just perfect for Albert, but he wants you to see it first. Come and look."

"Yes, Yes, I will look," Rurrik let Margaret lead him through the store to the pre-teen section.

The suit was black sharkskin with greenish-gold undertones. Prince Albert put on the jacket and windmilled his arms to check for mobility. "We have nothing like this in Russia," Rurrik stammered as his voice began to return.

"No sharkskin?" Margaret asked as she helped Albert out of the jacket.

Rurrik looked for the first time at the suit. He held up one of the jacket sleeves and let it roll back and forth on his fingers. The light played off the fabric turning it first black and then green gold. "No, no sharkskin."

"Come help us pick out a shirt," Margaret said as she flipped through several shelves stacked high with luminous shirts. She held up first one and then another before settling on a cotton candy pink synthetic number. Rurrik was getting his sea legs and picked out a narrow, pink and green striped tie that set off both the shirt and the suit.

"Do you have relatives in China?" Rurrik asked while Prince Albert was in the dressing room trying on the suit pants. He was not a natural conversationalist in any language, but he hoped to avoid conversations about Russia by talking about China.

"I'm sure I do but I'm afraid that connection was lost when my parents died. Do you have much family in Russia?"

"No," Rurrik said in defeat. His mind angled for another question.

Prince Albert returned just in time. He looked dapper in his new suit. Next, they turned their attention to Rurrik. At first, he put up some resistance, but Margaret and Albert softened him and finally decked him out in a charcoal gray, hound's-tooth jacket with square cut, black velour lapels, and pocket flaps, an electric blue Dacron shirt that brought out his eyes, and a narrow velour tie. The one item Rurrik insisted on, the garment most prized by the youth of Russia, was a pair of genuine Levi Straus jeans fastened at the waist by a wide black garrison belt. There was a little money left over and Prince Albert used it to buy Margaret a sweater clip.

When the shopping spree was over, The Prince and Rurrik dropped Margaret off around the corner from her house. "Better my aunt doesn't see me riding in a car with boys, particularly two such fine dressers. You know how to get back from here now, don't you?" Margaret asked.

"Four blocks to Union and then left. Straight up Union and we see Taylor's," Rurrik recited.

"You will need to find Ma Atherton's. Go past the Memphis Recording Service and turn right down Myrtle Street. Ma Atherton's rooming house is the last one before the railroad tracks," Margaret added.

"Will you come to recording session tonight? Rurrik asked.

"I'm not sure if my aunt will approve, but I'm not sure that will stop me either. Whether I make it or not you should come back to Taylor's in the morning. I'll fix you up with some biscuits and gravy," Margaret offered.

"Same gravy?"

"I'm afraid so, but the biscuits are the best in town."

"I will be there," Rurrik promised.

CHAPTER 13

The two sharply dressed friends followed the directions back up Union Avenue and down Myrtle Street to the rooming house. It was old and close to the tracks, but it appeared to be well maintained. Ma Atherton was sitting in the parlor and expecting the two. After remarking on how handsome Prince Albert looked, she informed them that they would find Gizmo on the second floor, which they did. The room was neat and clean, with twin beds and a cot for Albert. "I was just about ready to head back over to the studio. You gentlemen wouldn't want to join me, would you?" Gizmo asked.

The evening air was crisp and clean, and the three friends decided to leave the car at the boarding house and walk back over to the recording service. The studio itself was much larger than it appeared from the outside. Rurrik helped the band carry equipment in the back door and set up while Sam Phillips, Gizmo, and Fats fooled around with recording levels in the control room. When things were set the band ran through the first number. Fats, Gizmo, and the band warmed to the task and soon the studio was rocking. Muscadine, Prince Albert, and

Rurrik sat in a row of folding chairs along one wall of the staging area.

Around eight, the night waitresses from Taylor's came in with trays of sandwiches, a jug of coffee, and a big glass of milk for Prince Albert. The combo took a break and Sam Phillips handed out cold bottles of beer from the refrigerator in his office. It was warm in the studio and Rurrik drank down his beer almost without stopping.

After the break, Fats and the band began to play *Walking to New Orleans*, one of Domino's signature pieces. About sixteen bars into the first take Rurrik let out a belch that caused the needles on the dials in the control room to bounce. The musicians pelted him with wadded-up sheets of music and crusts of bread from the sandwiches.

The merriment ended suddenly when the door to the studio opened, and Margaret Soo walked in. She no longer wore her waitress uniform but an oriental dress of jade green with bamboo and cherry blossoms embroidered in gold and red. She also wore lipstick and eyeliner. Her hair was not in a ponytail but hung long and silky down her back. Rurrik could not take his eyes off her as she took a seat in one of the folding chairs.

The band began the song from the top and Margaret smiled over at Rurrik. The young mariner sat with his mouth agape. Prince Albert jabbed the Russian hard in the ribs and pointed with his thumb in the direction of Margaret. Rurrik snapped out of his trance and, walking over to the new arrival, offered her his hand. The Russian defector and the Chinese-American waitress danced together through *Walking to New Orleans* and two takes of *Can I Walk You Home*. Rurrik's breathing was shallow, and his lungs hurt. His ears were ringing, and the top of his head threatened to float away. Despite these maladies, he was able to glide around the small space in perfect time.

"How you holdin' up?" Gizmo asked the Prince.

Prince Albert, who was slumped in a chair with a half-eaten sandwich hanging from his mouth, straightened and smiled. He propped his eyes open to show how awake he was but none of the musicians were convinced.

"Rurrik, I hate to break up this perfect duet, but would you mind taking the Prince here back to Ma Atherton's?" Gizmo asked. "Get him settled and then come on back if you like."

"I'll go with you for company," Margaret offered.

Margaret and the two hoofers walked back up Union then turned down Myrtle Street. The night air was chilly now and Rurrik gave Margaret his greatcoat for warmth. They hummed Domino's tunes as they went. When they got to the rooming house Rurrik left Margaret in the parlor with Ma Atherton and took Albert up the stairs. The Prince got ready for bed and was asleep as soon as his head hit the pillow. Rurrik quietly pulled the door closed behind him as he left the room.

Back down in the parlor, Margaret was telling Ma Atherton about Rurrik and the Multimixer. "Is only good for short time," Rurrik said apologetically.

"Ma comes in every Saturday for a Malt," Margaret explained.

"Lots of vitamins in malt," Ma Atherton informed him.

"Then you will to get one," Rurrik said with confidence. "But now we must go back to studio."

"I'll look in on the Prince but you best take a key with you," Ma said as she took a key from her apron pocket and handed it to Rurrik. "I'm going to bed right after Steve Allen."

Out on the street, Rurrik started toward the car but changed his mind. "The car can be very much loud."

Margaret took him by the arm. "If we walk by the tracks, it will take us to an alley that comes out right across from the studio. It's a lot quicker," she said. "I wouldn't go this way at night if I were alone, but I feel safe in the company of the Russian Navy."

"Merchant Marines," Rurrik corrected.

The passage was darker than he had expected and made precarious by all manner of boxes, garbage cans, discarded items of furniture, and automobiles from another era. Margaret walked with ease, but it took concentration on the part of the young Russian. He did not want to stumble over unseen garbage cans and wake the people whose bedroom windows faced the alley.

Ahead of them, Rurrik could see the lights from Union Avenue, and he used this as a beacon. He also saw something that caused him to freeze in his tracks. There were two men in heavy coats and wide-brimmed hats standing in the shadows at the mouth of the alley. One was tall and the other short and stocky. They seemed to be watching Taylor's and the front of the Memphis Recording Studio which was, as predicted, directly across Union. The young mariner grabbed Margaret by the arm and pulled her down into the blackness behind a rusting Packard.

"Who are those men and why are we hiding from them?" Margaret asked in a whisper.

"I believe they are known to me. I believe is Sergeant Kostonka and Officer Bolachko."

"Friends of yours?" Margaret said with a touch of sarcasm.

"Not friends. I know them to be Moscow police, but I fear they are now KGB."

"KGB?"

"Russian secret police."

"Russian secret police?" Margaret said in disbelief. "What are they doing here in Memphis?"

"There is something I must tell you," Rurrik confessed. "I am not in Russian Navy."

"You're in the Merchant Marines, you already confessed that."

"I am not in Merchant Marine either, I am defector. But not even that, I am a spy."

"A spy? A Russian spy?"

"Yes, yes a spy," Rurrik hung his head.

"What are you spying on, American Rock & Roll?" Margaret laughed.

"It is truth. My government wants to encourage Rock & Roll. I was sent here to find out how we can do such."

"Encourage Rock & Roll?"

"Your government thinks that it will corrupt youth of America. My government wants to help to bring about corruption."

"So, you are a Rock & Roll spy, sent here to encourage the corruption of the youth of America."

"Yes," Rurrik said dejectedly. "I am so embarrassed to tell you this because I like you very much and now you know I am Russian spy."

"A Russian spy sent here to promote Rock & Roll and corrupt the youth of America."

"Yes."

"On behalf of the youth of America, I want to thank you from the bottom of my heart," Margaret said as she kissed the young Russian full on the lips. Taken by surprise, Rurrik's legs stiffened and, as they did, one of his shoes struck a garbage can. A young raccoon leaped from the can, and scurried across the alley and down a storm drain. The two men turned quickly toward the sound and looked in the direction of the Packard.

"What in blue blazes," the tall man at the end of the alley exclaimed in English as the coon disappeared down the drain. "Biggest Goddamn rat I've ever seen."

"That wasn't a rat, it was a raccoon," the stocky man explained. "He probably lives in the brush along the tracks. Feeds on the garbage in the alley at night."

"Rats, coons, snakes, alligators, ticks, chiggers. I don't know how you do it, Peal. This Goddamn part of the country ain't fit to live in."

"Now hold on Van Pelt. You got raccoons in DC just like we do down here. They were all over Quantico when I was up there for training. I've seen dead raccoons on Rock Creek Parkway as far down as the Lincoln Memorial," Peal pointed out.

Back behind the Packard Margaret turned to Rurrik and whispered, "Let's start over, shall we? Who did you say those men were?"

Rurrik turned his hands palm up and shook his head

At the mouth of the alley, Van Pelt continued his review of southern fauna. "How about alligators? How about them? You ever see any alligators in Washington? And cotton mouths and water moccasins and brown recluse spiders, how about them,

Peal? We don't have any of them in Georgetown. And these rednecks, coon asses, and peckerwoods, and the food they eat. Roast beef cooked as dark as shoe leather, breakfast sausage on the pizza. This is the only place I've ever been to that considers macaroni and cheese a vegetable. I can't wait to get this mission over with and my rear end back to civilization."

"I don't feel sorry for you in the least," Peal answered. "You brought this on yourself."

"Now, how do you figure that?"

"You know what your problem is? You do your job too well. Now me, I try and coffee-break my way through each day. I do what I have to do to get by, but I found out early on that if you do more than expected The Bureau will just expect more of you."

"Oh, is that my problem?"

"As soon as my boss heard about the work you did in Europe with the Penniman plane he was on the phone to your boss and your fate was sealed. On the other hand, your boss has never heard my name and never will if I can help it."

"I thought we were going to have another plane down here for me to work on?"

"We thought so as well. But we got a man on the inside. It sounds like the Fat Man has seen the light. He's done with Rock & Roll."

"Maybe we should take him down just to be on the safe side?"

"See what I mean about you being an over-achiever?" Peal said. "All we got to do is dispose of the master tapes here at Sun, and then take care of Holly wherever the hell he is."

"Does Holly have a plane I can work on?" Van Pelt said with anticipation.

"Sorry, no plane. He's out in the Midwest somewhere on a bus tour. How are you with buses?"

"No challenge to a bus. Heck, half the time they break down all by themselves," Van Pelt observed.

"How did you pull that off with Penniman over there? Having that plane catch fire but not crash. Mission accomplished, no dead bodies, no investigations. That was the hand of an artist at work," Peal said with admiration.

"Artist? Wasn't no art to it. I was trying to bring that plane down in flames. Get rid of that freak of nature and his whole band," Van Pelt gestured toward Sun Records. "What do you say we hit the fat man while we're here, make all this alley squattin' worthwhile?"

"We got our orders, destroy the tape and then put Holly out of commission and that's it," Peal stated.

"OK, but if four eyes gets on a plane out there in the heartland his butt is mine.

Margaret took Rurrik by the arm and the two started to ease backward through a dilapidated wooden gate and into one of the small backyards that opened onto the alley. A rather large dog that was chained in the small yard awoke and voiced his objections. The dog's snarling bark sent all manner of small creatures skittering across the alley. Margaret and Rurrik dashed back through the gate and flattened once again behind the Packard.

Peal and Van Pelt drew revolvers from beneath their coats and peered into the darkness of the alley. "We should check this out," Peal said.

Margaret and Rurrik clung to each other and tried to make themselves invisible against the rusted car.

Van Pelt holstered his weapon. "You can go back into that menagerie if you want to but I'm going to find a vantage point that offers a little more civilization."

"You might be right," Peal agreed as he holstered his pistol as well. "There's a drug store on the corner of the next block. We can get a cup of coffee and still watch the studio."

Margaret and Rurrik waited until they were sure the two men were gone and then began to make their way back down the alley in the direction they had come from.

Margaret took Rurrik by the arm. "We have to get to Sam and Fats."

Rurrik balked. "Those men had guns."

"We can follow the tracks down to Monroe and come up behind the studio."

"They are watching the studio. Those men, they had guns."

"Focus, Rurrik," Margaret propelled the young Russian down the embankment and onto the tracks.

It took quite some time to negotiate the railroad track in the dark and the embankment up onto Monroe Street was steep and slick. By the time they got to the parking lot behind the Memphis Recording Service, both Margaret and Rurrik were covered with mud, scratches, and beggar's lice.

Rurrik tried the nob of the studio's heavy metal door. It was locked.

"They'll be at Taylor's," Margret said

She was right. The two businesses shared the parking lot and the back door to Taylor's was open. Fats, Muscadine, Gizmo, Sam Phillips, and most of the band sat around the tables drinking coffee and beer. The two new arrivals joined Sam and Gizmo at a small table near the door.

"My southern upbringing forbids me to ask what you two have been up to," Sam said.

"And just look at you," Gizmo said. "Next time ask me and I'll give you money for a room."

Rurrik composed himself as best he could. "There were two men, two men with guns. They watch studio from alley."

165

"We had to go down the tracks and come up Monroe so they wouldn't see us," Margaret added.

Gizmo laughed. "Conspiracy theory, that would be Fats' department."

"Two men from The Bureau," Margaret said.

"The Bureau?" Sam asked.

"KGB, only American," Rurrik replied.

"They were FBI. One of them sabotaged Little Richard's plane in Europe," Margaret added.

"Why don't the two of you sit down and have a beer? Look, I made you a copy of the session." Sam slid a round metal tape canister across the counter. "We finished it up tonight. That's the whole thing, Elvis, Buddy Holly, Jerry Lee, Carl Perkins, all of them You can take it back to Russia with you if you ever decide to return.

"Damn, I left my copy in the studio," Gizmo exclaimed as he got to his feet. "Let me have your key Sam, so I can go back and get it right now before I forget it entirely."

Sam got to his feet as well. "You better let me go with you. That lock is tricky."

Rurrik put his hand on Gizmo's arm. "The men with guns."

"Right, men with the guns," Gizmo said as he and Sam left the cafe. "Standard-issue American KGB guns, I'm sure."

Margaret and Rurrik moved to the table where Fats and Muscadine sat along with Joey Cicero and several other musicians. The tabletop was littered with empty and part-empty beer bottles.

"They are here," Rurrik said.

"Who are here?" Fats asked.

"The two men from behind theater in New Orleans," Rurrik said.

Margaret joined in. "They were across the street in the alley. And they have guns."

Muscadine pulled back his jacket exposing a revolver in a shoulder holster. "Don't you worry, young lady, we got guns too."

"We have to stop them. They are going to destroy the tapes and then Buddy," Margaret said.

Muscadine rose from the table. "And you say they are across the street in the alley,"

"They are not there now. They have gone for coffee," Rurrik said.

Fats pulled Muscadine back down into his seat. "Gone for coffee?"

And then it happened. Time stopped. Fats, Margaret, Rurrik, Muscadine, and all within the cafe hung in suspended animation. A white flash, visible through the windows, lit up the parking lot behind Taylor's. The air within the cafe seemed to suck back toward the rear of the building and then rush forward. A wave of sound shook the walls, rattling the windows

and the glasses on the shelves behind the counter and sending
beer bottles spinning across the table. The inside of the cafe
went dark.

CHAPTER 14

Rurrik and Muscadine were among the first out the door and into the lot. Shards of broken glass were everywhere. Both the door and rear windows of Memphis Recording Service were gone, and flames licked from the empty frames. Gizmo, Sam, and the studio's metal door lay in the dirt. None of the three were in very good shape.

"Call an ambulance," Muscadine yelled back over his shoulder as he hurried to aid Sam Philips who was trying to stand. Sam got as far as one knee and fell forward. Muscadine caught him just before he hit the dirt.

Rurrik rushed to Gizmo's motionless body. He checked for a pulse but could not find it. He put his head on the older man's chest and listened for a heartbeat. Muscadine left Sam Phillips in the hands of the other musicians and joined Rurrik and Margaret at Gizmo's side. The ex-boxer knelt by the musician's head. "Is his airway clear?"

"I do not know," Rurrik took the old musician's hand. "Gizmo, I will not leave you."

Margaret grabbed Rurrik by the arm and pulled him aside. "You're a Russian spy. You can't be here when the police arrive."

"But Gizmo, he is my friend," Rurrik said.

Muscadine looked up at Margaret and Rurrik. "He's still breathin'."

Margaret spun Rurrik around and looked him straight in the eyes. "Baptist Hospital is four blocks away. Listen, you can hear the sirens already." Rurrik nodded his head. He could hear the sirens.

"There is nothing we can do right now. If he can be saved, they will save him. We have to get you out of here before the police arrive. These people who did this are going after Buddy next. You can't help Gizmo here and you can't help anybody if you're in jail."

"Should somebody tell the police about the men in the alley?" Rurrik asked

"Maybe somebody should, but not us. Do you know who The Bureau is? The Bureau is the Federal Bureau of Investigation. FBI, it rhymes with KGB. Now if we go to the police, it will be the word of a Chinese waitress and a Russian spy against the word of J. Edgar Hoover. Who do you think they are more likely to believe?"

Rurrik knew she was right, "But we must get Prince Albert," Rurrik insisted. The sirens were much louder now, and a second set of more distant sirens could be heard coming from the direction of downtown.

"The cops will be here any second," Margaret said. "Fats will take care of the Prince."

An ambulance pulled into the alley and Muscadine parted the growing crowd. The medics went quickly about their work and had Sam and Gizmo on gurneys and loaded into the ambulance in a matter of minutes. As they closed the door on the back of the wagon, Rurrik could see that Sam was trying to sit up. Gizmo was motionless. Muscadine cleared an exit path for the ambulance, and it disappeared down the alley.

Margaret and Rurrik looked around for Fats. They found him standing and looking through the blackened doorway into the gutted studio. The flames had died down, but crackling bursts of blue electric light flashed in the interior. Black, acrid smoke rolled across the ceiling and out into the night air. "They must have been foolin' with the lock when the place blew. That metal door kept them from being burnt to a crisp," the fat man shook his head. "Why, why do this? It's only music."

"These people are serious," Muscadine said as he joined the group.

Margaret appealed to the fat man. "We have to find Buddy and warn him."

"He's somewhere up north, Wisconsin or maybe Minnesota. The only places I know up there are Chicago and Detroit." Fats said, "I can make some calls and find out."

"We can rent a car in the morning," Muscadine said

"No. You can't go," Margaret said. "They expect you to go back to New Orleans. Right now, we have the advantage. We know where they are going next and what they plan to do. If you two go they'll know for sure we're on to them. We might save Buddy but, on the other hand, we might lose you. Rurrik and I will have to go."

"I guess you're right about that. Two big black men with silk suits and southern accents would tend to stand out up there in the corn belt," Fats said in resignation and then turned toward Rurrik. "What can I do to help?" The young Russian, still somewhat in shock, stared blankly after the ambulance.

"Could you take care of Prince Albert?" Margaret asked.

"Don't even have to ask," Fats took a wad of bills out of his pocket and handed it to Margaret.

A fire truck and two police cars pulled into the lot. The four friends moved away from the rear of the studio and eased over by the back door to the cafe. Rurrik could not take his eyes from the parking lot and stumbled on the steps. Muscadine took out his pistol and handed it to Rurrik. The Russian looked down at the heavy handgun but made no attempt to take it.

172

"Keep it out of sight, you know, don't let the cops see it," Muscadine instructed. "And don't use it if you don't have to."

Rurrik continued to stare at the revolver but still made no attempt to take it.

"We can't let the police question Rurrik," Margaret said.

"You a wanted man, Rurrik?" Muscadine asked.

"He's a Russian defector," Margaret explained.

"Is that a bad thing, or a good thing?" Fats asked.

There were now several cops in the parking lot, and they were organizing the crowd for questioning. "You got to get out of here," Muscadine stuffed the revolver down into the pocket of the greatcoat that Margaret still wore. "And you gotta take our Russian friend with you and hope he snaps out of it."

Margaret took Rurrik by the arm and the two slipped into Taylor's, locking the door behind them as they went. The fire in the recording studio had cut off the electricity to the cafe as well. The only illumination in the dining area came from the streetlight in front of the building and the flashing red lights on the police and fire vehicles which shone in the back. The place was in ruin. Chairs and tables had been tipped and everything spilled onto the floor. The two had to pick their way carefully in the-semi darkness. At the front door, Rurrik stopped. He looked around at the destruction and then down at Margaret. He seemed to focus for the first time. "We have to get the tape."

"The tape?"

"It is last one. We cannot let them get it."

In the dim light, he picked his way back to the table where Sam Phillips and Gizmo had been. The corner was dark, and the table had been turned over in the sudden exodus following the blast. He could hear somebody rattling the knob of the back door. Rurrik got down on his hands and knees and began to feel around in the darkness for the tape. He found it among the plates and ashtrays and joined Margaret who waited by the front door.

"We can't take it with us. If they grab us, they get the tape also. We can't take that chance," Margaret said.

Rurrik worked his way back behind the counter and lifted the cover off the Multimixer. He put the metal tape box in on top of the drive wheel and then pressed the cover firmly back in place. The knob rattling stopped and Fats and Muscadine could be heard talking to a police officer. Rurrik, without the tape, hurried back to where Margaret waited at the front door. Once again, he balked. "Poster. I must get poster."

The knob rattling started again but this time with much more force. The young Russian danced around the fallen chairs and back behind the counter once more. Outside the back door of the café, the knob rattler lost patience and began pounding on the door with a fist. Rurrik tore the Winter Dance Party poster from the wall. The door pounding was embellished with cussing as Rurrik dove over the counter. He took Margaret by the arm and the two hurried out the front door as the back door frame splintered. The two fugitives ran across the street and into the safety of the alley's shadows.

On Myrtle Street, they found Gizmo's car where Rurrik had left it. They waited long enough to regain their composure and then drove around the corner and back down Union Avenue past the dark windows of Taylor's Cafe. After a few miles Rurrik saw a sign for Highway 51 and turned north. On the seat between them lay the poster that the young Russian had taken risks to retrieve. Margaret picked it up. "You picked a fine time to go souvenir hunting," she remarked.

Rurrik slowed the car beneath a streetlight. "Look at below."

At the bottom of the poster, in smaller print, were the dates and locations of the stops on the tour. "February 2nd," Margaret read. "Surf Ballroom, Clear Lake, Iowa."

In the darkness they crossed out of Tennessee and into Kentucky. Just after three in the morning the old DeSoto climbed up the east side of the long, rainbow shaped bridge that carried travelers across the Ohio River and out of Kentucky. The engine was running hot and moisture was beading down the inside of the windshield. The car crawled across the apex of the arch and rolled down the west side of the bridge and into Cairo, Illinois, a farming town of no great consequence. Rurrik looked for a service station but the only one he saw was closed. He pulled the car in beside the pumps and turned the engine off.

The former mechanic opened the hood and looked in at the engine. Water was leaking from the faulty heater valve and turning to steam on the hot exhaust manifold. "We will have to let it cool before I can fix."

"How's the gas?"

"Empty."

The two got back into the car and huddled beneath the greatcoat. At six thirty Margaret shook Rurrik awake. "The lights are on at the cafe down the block, and I just saw some people go in."

They got out of the car, cold and stiff and walked to the cafe. In the light from the door Margaret counted the money that Fats had given her so casually. She was surprised to find it to be nearly three hundred dollars.

They asked the woman behind the cash register about the gas station and found out it would open at 7:00 AM or thereabouts, depending on when the attendant arrived. They ordered some sausage biscuits and coffee. Every eye in the place was on them as they waited for their order. "I guess they don't see many Chinese in formal dress dining with Russian spies here in Cairo," Margaret said.

The farm supply store next door opened at 7 sharp. Margaret dashed up and down the aisles picking up jeans for herself and work shirts for them both. She also picked up wool sweaters and socks, work boots, and warm fleece lined jackets. Rurrik noticed a large, vinyl lined, pouch-like pocket in the back of his jacket and stuck his hand in one side and out the other.

"That's for squirrel hunting," the clerk explained. "You put the dead squirrels in the pouch so's to have both hands free for your gun. That little slot above the pocket on the front is for your hunting license."

"Is there a place here I can change?" Margaret asked.

The clerk pointed her to a small office in the back and she hurried off. "Never seen a woman shop as fast as that. She's a keeper."

Gloves, hats and two warm woolen blankets rounded out the ensemble. "This should help us blend in with the general population," Margaret said as she spun quickly around, modeling her new wardrobe.

The service station attendant was just arriving when they got back to the car. Rurrik rolled up their old clothes in the greatcoat and threw them into the trunk of the car. While the attendant pumped the gas, the young Russian saw to the engine. The heater valve was shot, and he borrowed a pocket knife from the attendant and cut it from the system. He looped the heater hose back to the engine rendering the heater useless but bypassing the leak. He got a can of water from the station and refilled the radiator. "It will run but we have no heat."

Rurrik paid for the gas and bought two quarts of oil, one of which he added to the engine. He got a free plastic bank in the shape of a car and a map of Illinois to add to the collection in the back seat as well as a map of Missouri which they kept in the front with them.

They left Cairo and climbed up and over the second, even longer, bridge that took them across the Mississippi River and into Missouri. The land here was flat, as flat as the Mississippi Delta but it looked to be a little more prosperous. Within a few miles, they reunited with Route 61 and stopped to change drivers. Margaret got behind the wheel and turned the car north toward Saint Louis.

At Barnhart they changed drivers again and, with Margaret reading the map, made their way west of St. Louis to Jefferson City. There they picked up Route 63 and Margaret slept while Rurrik followed the road to the north through seemingly identical small towns. In Westville, Rurrik stopped again for gas. The wind reminded him of Moscow, and he could feel the cold work its way in around the car door. To the west, the sun was ringed by an icy circle with a bright sun dog along the northern rim. To the north, the sky was dropping down like a heavy gray blanket.

"What are you looking at?" Margaret asked as she rubbed the sleep from her eyes.

"I don't know about America but in Russia a sky like that means snow."

Rurrik paid the attendant and got a free map of Iowa, a mechanical pencil with the name of the station, an ashtray in the shape of a tire, and a key chain. Rurrik put them in the back seat along with the other treasures. From a machine inside the station, Margaret got two cardboard cups of coffee. The road was straight here and the traffic light as Margaret took over behind the wheel. The wind, gusty and from the northwest now, set the car gently rocking like a ship at sea. The young Mariner, despite the coffee, fell immediately into a deep sleep.

After a time Rurrik began to dream and in his dream, he was back in the cell in the basement of the Moscow Police Station. It was cold and damp and he was completely alone. He heard once again the water dripping in the drainpipe and the running toilet and then he heard a new sound. A tapping sound, perhaps a code, was coming from the next cell. He focused on the sound but could not make sense of it.

He tried to lift his head, but it was too heavy. His arms would not respond. He was paralyzed. The tapping sound grew louder and closer. It wasn't from the next cell but from outside the door. He opened his mouth and willed himself to speak, to ask who was there, but nothing came out. Rurrik mustered all his power and shouted. "Stay away from my door!"

"Rurrik! Are you alright?"

Rurrik woke and quickly gathered his wits. "I was dreaming. I was back in Moscow and..." The tapping sound was still there. It had not gone away with the rest of the dream. "Slow down."

Margaret slowed the car and the tapping sound slowed as well but steam came up from under the hood.

"How far to the next town?" Rurrik asked.

"Two miles to Prospect. What do we do?"

"Drive slow and pray."

CHAPTER 15

The knocking sound grew louder but the DeSoto made it to the outskirts of Prospect. They could see most of the town from the highway as they passed through. There was only one gas station that had service bays and it was closed.

"Pull in any way," Rurrik said. "The least we need is water."

Rurrik got out, opened the hood, and disappeared in a plume of steam. When the steam dissipated, he looked into the engine compartment and then lay down and stuck his head under the front of the car. "Is lower radiator hose."

"Can you fix it with a knife like you did the heater hose?"

Rurrik shook his head in defeat. "Maybe, if just one part bad, but it is rotted."

"What do we do?"

"I do not know."

"We can't just quit. We have to warn Buddy and the rest."

As she spoke, they became aware of the fact that they were listening to music; Rock & Roll music. It was faint but coming from the back of the station. They followed the sound and saw a lean-to extension behind the garage. A light burned in the window. Margaret knocked on the unpainted wooden door and then knocked again with force. The music stopped and a tall thin teenager with a guitar in his hand opened the door. "Excuse our interruption but we are having a problem with our car," Margaret said.

"The station opens at seven in the morning," the thin youth replied. "Just leave it out front and we'll get to it first thing."

Behind the teen, Margaret could see a bass player and a drummer. On a table against the wall were a record player, records, and a stack of Rock & Roll fan magazines. It was a scene repeated in countless garages, basements, and back bedrooms across America. The boys were playing the records over and over again while trying to learn a bass line, a drum riff, or a guitar solo.

"But we have to get to Clear Lake tonight," she said.

Behind the guitar man. the drummer spoke. "If you're going to see Buddy Holly, you best forget it. If you don't have tickets, you won't get in. It's a sell-out."

"We have to get there to warn Buddy," Margaret pleaded.

"Warn him about what?" the thin teen asked.

"The FBI is to stop Buddy Holly from making the Rock & Roll music," Rurrik stepped forward and said in his heavy Russian accent.

The drummer laughed, "You're not from around here, are you?"

Margaret pushed Rurrik aside. "Buddy is in danger. Look, I'm Margaret Soo, the waitress at Taylor's, the cafe next to Sun Records, and, well, this is hard to explain, but it is very important that we get to Clear Lake tonight."

The guitar man looked suspiciously at Rurrik who was thumbing through the Rock & Roll magazines on the table.

"It's my dad's garage and he would be pretty mad if he caught me in there at night messing with his tools and stuff,"

"But if we don't get there ..." Margaret pleaded.

Rurrik flipped one of the magazines open and handed it to the bass player.

"Good Golly, Miss Molly! It's her!" the bass player blurted out. "That's her right there with Elvis!"

It was the photo of Elvis and Sam Phillips drinking coffee in Taylor's. The same photo that Rurrik kept in his pocket. Between the two, topping off Elvis's cup was Margaret.

"This is for real?" the guitar man asked.

"It's very important," Margaret said.

"Ain't a car we can't fix," the drummer said as the three hastily donned coats, bolted from the lean-to, and scurried around to the front of the garage.

"Is lower radiator hose," Rurrik said as the three teens swarmed over the car.

"It's the lower radiator hose," the bass player said as he looked out from under the front of the car.

"You two go get some coffee and we will have this running in no time. Half an hour, tops," the guitar man advised.

"I could use some coffee and some food too," Margaret said.

The guitar man did not take his eyes off the job at hand. "Two blocks down to the public square. Woolworth on your right. The Central Cafe is just across from the courthouse door. Try the loose-meat sandwich, house special. We'll bring the car by as soon as we are finished."

Margaret and Rurrik found the Central Cafe without a problem. It was neat and clean and well-lit. They settled into a booth and waited for the waitress. Margaret spun the table jukebox and looked at the selections. "I don't know what will happen if they kill Rock & Roll. All we'll be left with is Fabian and a lot of guys named Bobby. I was fifteen when my parents died, and my aunt took me in. New family, new school; everything was so foreign. I felt lost until I got the job at Taylor's and found Rock & Roll. My aunt and her husband are good people but very Chinese. Their ways are centuries old. Their house is large but there was no place for me there. I wanted to be an American."

The waitress came and Margaret ordered the loose-meat sandwich, fries, and a Coke.

"I'll have the meat sandwich and Coke also, and do you have beans and rice?" Rurrik asked.

"I believe we do," the waitress said as she left.

184

"When I was in school all was classical music," Rurrik explained. "I left academy after my mother took ill and then, there was nothing. When I found American Rock & Roll it was all I had."

"And your mother?"

"She had stroke and never recovered. She die last fall."

"I'm so sorry, Rurrik," Margaret took his hand in hers.

The waitress placed the Cokes on the table. "Food will be out in a minute."

"I didn't know you had to go to school for this," Margaret asked.

"School for what?"

"Spy school. You said you were at the academy. Is that the Soviet spy school?"

"I studied for ballet. It was only new that I became spy. This was first assignment. It was plan to defect in New Orleans but then I meet Gizmo and things go, how you say, sideways. I don't know what will happen to me now. In your country, I am spy. Right now, I go to Clear Lake but after that, I don't know where I go"

"I don't suppose you can go back to Russia."

"I don't think so. I don't think I go back even if I could. There is very little light in my country."

"It's the latitude," Margaret explained. "In the winter you have less light, in the summer you have more. When one pole is

185

dark all day the other pole is light all night. Every place on earth averages the same. Half light, half dark."

"I do not mean sunlight. I am talk about hope."

"Everybody can hope for something, even Russians."

"In my country we only try survive. When we dare to hope it is a dark hope. In Russia it is very much hard to dream. It wears down the soul."

The waitress returned with the food order. Loose-meat sandwiches turned out to be simply ground beef, steamed and mounded on a hamburger bun. "Do you have any hot sauce, maybe some onion or a slice of tomato?" Margaret said as she pulled back the top of the bun.

"Ketchup on the table," the waitress said.

Rurrik looked down at his side orders; a small plate with cooked green beans and another with unadorned white rice. "This is not rice and beans I think it would be."

"Look around you. The people in this town are all white. Some of them are even whiter than you. I'm sure they are all decent people, but you can't expect much from the rice and beans in a place like this."

"I don't know where I go when this is over, but I don't think I stay in Iowa."

A few stray flakes of snow were falling on the sidewalks of Prospect as the garage band pulled the DeSoto to a stop in front of the Cafe'.

186

"We didn't have the right hose, but we made do with one from a Plymouth. We put some anti-freeze in there as well. You were running on pure water. That might be alright in Louisiana, but it wouldn't get you far in Iowa," the guitar man explained. "The heater is back working again but we didn't have a replacement for the valve. It was either on or off. We figured you're going to need the defroster, so we chose the on position. If you get too hot just open a window. The tank is full."

The three musicians lined up like Magi and lavished the two travelers with gifts: an ice scraper with the name of the garage on it, a second bank, this one in the shape of a gas pump, and a set of pink and black foam rubber dice.

"Hang them from your rear-view mirror for luck," the guitar man said of the dice.

Rurrik thanked the boys and Margaret offered them some money which they declined. She folded some bills and put them in the guitar man's jacket pocket. "Buy a few Sun Records. I hear they're coming out with a Rock & Roll super set. Double album."

It was past midnight when they reached Clear Lake. Despite the lightly falling snow, several carloads of teens were still parked in the lot beside the Surf Ballroom. The car engines were running but the windows were open as cigarettes and pint bottles were passed back and forth between the vehicles.

Rurrik pulled up alongside one of the cars and rolled his window down. "The concert, it is over?" he asked a redheaded teen with a sharp nose and a bad complexion who was sitting in the front passenger's seat.

"The concert it is, man," the teen replied.

"And Mr. Buddy Holly, he is gone?" Rurrik asked.

"He is way gone," the teen answered.

The rear window rolled down and a girl with dirty blond hair and gum in her braces joined the conversation. "Say, are you from Russia or someplace?"

Margaret leaned over and joined in. "We're from Memphis. How long has the concert been over?"

"I don't know," the redhead held up the pint and judged the level of its contents. "Half an hour, maybe a little more."

"There!" Rurrik pointed to the rear of the ballroom. A bus, with Winter Dance Party lettered on the side, pulled out from behind the building, traversed the edge of the parking lot, and started down the street.

"That's it!" Margaret said. "That's Buddy's bus."

Rurrik gunned the engine, popped the clutch, and spun the wheel. The old car slid in a half circle throwing a rooster tail of slush out behind the drive wheel and over the parked car. The DeSoto fishtailed as Rurrik brought it back under control. At the edge of town, they caught up with the band. Passing the bus, he once again spun the wheel and slid the old car to a stop blocking the road. "Not bad, not bad at all," Margaret said as she pushed herself away from the dashboard.

"Moscow taxi cab," Rurrik explained.

Margaret jumped from the car and beat on the door of the bus with the palm of her hand. The driver opened the door and she bounded up the steps with Rurrik at her heels. "Now hold on a minute," the driver said as he barred the way with his arm.

"I must talk to Buddy," Margaret pleaded.

"We got a long trip and there ain't no room for fans," the driver stated flatly.

"That ain't no fan," a voice from the back of the bus said. "That's Margaret Soo from Taylor's."

"Who is Margaret Sue?" the driver asked still barring the way.

"You never heard of Peggy Soo?" The man from the back of the bus said as he made his way to the front.

"Peggy Sue, *The* Peggy Sue?"

"One and the same." the man from the back of the bus was now beside the driver. Margaret was delighted to recognize Waylon, a young Memphis session musician who had been in Taylor's often.

"What are you doing in the middle of Iowa in the middle of the night and in the middle of a blizzard?" he asked.

"Waylon, where is Buddy? We have to warn him."

"He's not on the bus," Waylon explained.

189

"We need to find him, he could be in danger,"

"What kind of danger?" Waylon asked.

"Two men are after him. Two men from the FBI. They're out to stop him from playing ever again."

"Well, they're not going to stop him on this bus, he's flying to Fargo," the bus driver said.

"Flying? On an airplane?" Rurrik said as his complexion turned a shade whiter than it already was.

"Buddy chartered a plane. Hell, I'd be on it myself, but Jape came down with the flu and I gave him my seat. They're at the airport now," Waylon said.

"Where is the airport?" Margaret said in desperation.

"Back the way you came, turn left in the middle of town. That's the Mason City Highway," the driver said. "About a mile and a half out you'll see Airport Road on the right. Turn at the Dekalb sign."

Margaret and Rurrik bounded down the steps and skated back to their car. The snowstorm was gaining momentum and the road was now covered in white. Inside the car, Rurrik slipped the lever into reverse, gunned the engine, and spun out into the road heading back toward town.

"What is Dekalb?" he asked as they sped through the deserted town and skidded onto the Mason City highway.

"Farm products, seeds, bug killers, fertilizer, and such. Look for a big ear of corn with wings."

"Winged corn?" Rurrik questioned.

"The Greeks had winged Pegasus, the Romans had Mercury, in America, we have winged corn."

"This is marvelous country," Rurrik observed.

"There it is, hard right!"

Rurrik slid the DeSoto in a power drift and churned the old car through the turn and down the road toward the airport. The ride was much rougher now but the traction somewhat better. "This road, it is dirt," Rurrik said. The surface itself could not be seen but there were recent tire tracks to follow. "These tracks in front, they are new. Perhaps we are not too late."

Up ahead, Margaret and Rurrik could see the lights from the runway. The airport wasn't much, just a base for crop dusters. There were two hangers made of corrugated tin and a Quonset hut for an operations building. These three structures along with a few gas tanks and the odd lean-to and outbuilding made up the total of the Mason City Airport. Two cars, illuminated by the light above the door, were parked in front of the Quonset hut but the windows of the building were dark. The snow was easing up and the flakes had become large and fluffy.

As they neared the Quonset hut Margaret and Rurrik heard a buzz that quickly built to a roar. Rurrik hit the brakes and the car slid sideways. A small, single-engine plane took off from the runway, banked hard, came back over the hangers and the Quonset hut then disappeared into the night. The car skidded to a stop against one of the small outbuildings near a large gasoline storage tank. The motor stalled. The sound of the plane faded and the quiet of new snow fell over the scene.

"We are too late," Rurrik said as he let his forehead sag forward against the steering wheel.

Margaret got out of the car. "They must have a radio here. If we can figure out how to work it, we might be able to contact the pilot and have him come back."

Rurrik got out as well. "I know radio."

As they were just about to turn the corner to the front of the shed Rurrik grabbed Margaret's arm and pulled her down behind the storage tank.

Three men had stepped from the darkness of one of the hangers into the light of the parking lot. The first two were FBI agents Van Pelt and Peal from Memphis. Margaret and Rurrik could not see the face of the third man. He had his head down and was trying to light a cigarette.

"It's the two men from the alley across from Sun Studios," Margaret spoke in a whisper.

"Who is third?" Rurrik asked.

"I don't know," Margaret replied. "I can't see his face." Just then, the third man looked up and took a deep drag from his smoke. "Oh my God!" Margaret whispered. "It's Joey Cicero, Fats' new drummer."

"Perhaps they have taken him prisoner," Rurrik suggested.

"Prisoner. I don't think so," Margaret said, "He's working with them."

"But he is musician. I heard him play very good. He cannot be with them."

As if in confirmation of Margaret's suspicions, agent Peal put his arm around Joey's shoulder. "That's the last of them, Joey. Berry, Penniman, Presley, Perkins, all out of commission, one way or another."

Joey laughed a nervous laugh. "I don't know if I feel as good as I should about this. After all, they are musicians too."

Van Pelt was alternately looking down at his watch and then up in the direction of the departed plane. "Rock & Roll ain't music. Put apes in a room with drums and guitars and they could play that stuff."

"Van Pelt has a point." Peal said "You played drums in a big band. To do that took years of hard work and practice and talent. These kids today got no talent. Hell, Chuck Berry can't even tune his guitar. With this bunch out of the picture, the path is clear for the big bands to make a comeback. When this is all over and the story can finally be told you'll be a hero."

"Maybe you're right," Cicero said as he joined Van Pelt and looked in the direction of the departed plane.

"I know I'm right," Peal said. "Rock & Roll is dead now, we killed it, but it was going to die soon anyway. Fads like that don't last. All we did is help it into the grave. We nailed the coffin shut and saved a lot of innocent teenagers in the process."

"Rock & Roll is history," Van Pelt added.

"History that will never be told," Peal said. "What's left of those Super Session tapes back at Sun Studios wouldn't even make good charcoal."

"Did you get the one from the cafe?" Joey asked.

Van Pelt looked up from his watch. "One what from the cafe?"

Joey Cicero was still looking after the departed plane. "There was a tape of the Super Session in Taylor's. Phillips gave it to that Russian kid."

"There was a Russian in Taylor's?" Peal mused. "I'll be damned, the Russians were behind this after all."

Van Pelt took Joey by the arm and spun him around. "There was a tape in Taylor's, and you left it there."

"Hey, I didn't know you guys was going to blow up the whole block. The place went dark, and I got pushed out the door with everybody else,"

Peal separated the two men. "No problem. All we have to do is go back down to Memphis and get the tape."

Back behind the storage tank, Margaret turned to Rurrik. "We have to get to that tape before they do."

The two eased out from behind the gas tank and slipped back to the car. Rurrik started the engine up and put it in gear. The old DeSoto spun out from behind the shed and then stalled.

"Son of a ...," Peal exclaimed. "Who the Devil is that?"

"It's the girl from Taylor's and that Russian kid," Joey said. The three dashed back inside the hanger and, in a matter of seconds, a black sedan shot out of the darkness.

Rurrik turned the key and brought the old car back to life. He gunned the engine, and it stalled a second time. The black sedan was closing in. Van Pelt leaned out of the passenger's side window, gun in hand, and fired in the direction of the DeSoto. Rurrik could hear bullets hitting the trunk of the car and when he turned to look back, he saw that the gas storage tank had been struck as well. Aviation fuel sprayed out onto the snow.

The young Russian kissed his fingers for luck and then turned the key once more. The car started. Rurrik eased the gas pedal down slowly revving the engine and then, putting the car in gear, floored it. The DeSoto sprang forward as a ball of flame shot from the tailpipe. The fireball ignited the gas that was leaking from the punctured fuel storage tank and the whole thing exploded.

CHAPTER 16

The shock from the blast propelled the DeSoto forward like a surfer on a wave. Looking in the rear-view mirror, Rurrik could see the black sedan engulfed in a twenty-foot-high wall of flame and rolling black smoke. "Those men, they will die in that fire. We must help them."

Margaret was looking back also. "They shot at us, they tried to kill us!" But even as she spoke the black car emerged from the wall of smoke trailing bits of fire and sparks behind it.

Rurrik focused on the road ahead as the old DeSoto fan-tailed back out toward the highway. The agents in the sedan were close behind. "We are good on dirt, but they have better tires. It will not be so good when we get to pavement."

Margaret was still looking out through the rear window. The black sedan was about 100 yards behind. "We have to beat them. That tape is all we have left." It was when she turned back to the front that she saw the other set of headlights. They were off to the left and were moving on a collision course with the DeSoto. "What is that?"

Rurrik peered into the night. "The bus. It is Mr. Buddy Holly's bus."

The DeSoto and the bus closed in on the junction of Airport Road and the Mason City Highway. The DeSoto won the race but just by a hair. Rurrik spun the wheel before the old car hit the pavement. The DeSoto slid sideways in front of the bus. With the rear wheels spinning, the car slipped across the road and onto the shoulder on the far side. The slick tires dug into the gravel of the shoulder throwing a spray of small stones and snow over the front of the bus as Margaret and Rurrik sped back toward Clear Lake.

The bus hissed to a stop blocking Airport Road. Agent Peal, who was driving the black sedan, stood hard on the brakes and turned the steering wheel in an evasive maneuver. The car slid sideways and banged its driver's side hard against the bus and then bounced off. Van Pelt jumped from the passenger's seat, gun in hand, and threw two useless shots at the retreating DeSoto. Peal revved the engine of the black sedan. He worked the gear shift from drive to reverse and back to drive again but it was of no use. The crash had done little damage to the bus but had driven the rear fender of the car inward, puncturing the tire on the drive wheel.

Waylon and the driver climbed down from the bus and looked after the departed DeSoto. "Get that damn bus out of the way," Van Pelt shouted, waving both his gun and his badge. "We're in pursuit of suspects and you're interfering with federal agents."

Waylon looked down at the crumpled fender. "I think you may have a flat tire. We might-could help you change it and then you could get right after those fugitives."

"You bunch of crackers. You let them get away," Van Pelt stammered.

"Gosh, I sure am sorry," the driver said. "Do you want to ride with us? We'll go after them with the bus if you like."

"Go after them? In the bus?" Van Pelt was steaming.

"If you like," the driver said.

Peal rolled down the driver's window. "I'll radio ahead. They won't make it back to Memphis. We'll have them and the tape in a matter of hours."

"Let me help you with that," Waylon said as he reached into the black sedan and twisted the hand mike from Peal's grip. With a yank, he tore the hand mike loose from the dashboard. "Calling all cars, calling all cars," he said into the useless bit of equipment.

"You can't do that, that's government property," Peal said as he fumbled for his gun. He cleared the pistol from his coat, but it was too late. Waylon was now holding a large, western-style revolver in his free hand and it was pointed right at Peal's nose. Van Pelt spun and leveled his pistol at Waylon.

"Not a smart move," the driver pointed out as he nodded toward the bus. All the bus windows were now open, and a gun of some kind was pointing from nearly every opening.

199

"Why don't you just come on and go with us?" Waylon suggested. "Perhaps we can drop you off on our way back to Mason City. Maybe someplace that has a phone."

Van Pelt turned around, tore the hat from his head, and threw it down into the snow.

Margaret and Rurrik were fugitives now and thought it prudent to take the back roads. On top of that, they got lost twice and the DeSoto had to have its plugs cleaned again. It was several days before made it back to Memphis. There had been plenty of time for the two FBI agents to get back on the road and beat them back to Union Avenue.

With Rurrik at the wheel, they drove slowly past Taylor's and the Memphis Recording Service. Plywood had been hastily nailed over shattered windows and the outside of both buildings was blackened by smoke and streaked by rivulets of dirty water. The cafe was dark and forlorn. A warning sign was taped to the door courtesy of the Memphis Police Department. Rurrik circled several blocks looking for the dark sedan but did not see it. He selected a parking spot on Monroe Street as far from the corner streetlight as he could find.

"When the darkness is good, I will go in and get tape," Rurrik reached forward with his finger and flipped the foam rubber dice that hung from the rear-view mirror.

"I'll go with you," Margaret asserted.

"It would be better you wait here," Rurrik said. "Of what material are these dice made?"

"It's called foam rubber," Margaret explained as she took the dice down and compressed one in her fist. "It's used for cushions and padding. No matter how hard you try to crush it, the stuff just bounces back." She opened her fist and the die returned to its original shape. "I have to believe that Rock and Roll is the same way. They can't stop it even if they get that tape."

Rurrik took the dice from her hand and compressed them.

"I don't like this," Margaret said placing both her hands on the Russian's arm. "Those men could be anywhere. They could be in there with their guns just waiting for you. You don't have to do this you know. It's not your country; it's not your music, and don't tell me about your job as a spy."

Rurrik adjusted the driver's side mirror to bounce the last of the sun's rays off his face. He made a fist, compressing one of the die, and then released it. The die bounced back to its original shape. "This foaming rubber is stuff of marvel. Somewhere in America man discover how for making this new kind of rubber. Another man saw and he said it would be used for making dice to hang from mirror in car. In Russia we want first man but cannot tolerate second man. What we do not realize, they can be same man.

"Everybody in America believes that future will be better, and they will be part of better future. In Russia we can only hope that tomorrow will be better, but in hearts, we do not believe it is such.

"Rock and Roll is powerful force, more powerful than bomb. It can make difference in a world but even light of Rock and Roll can die in country like mine. If we let these men win, if we let them destroy tape and music, then your country becomes more like mine."

Margaret leaned over and kissed Rurrik square on the mouth. "You be careful in there."

Rurrik left the DeSoto and, staying in the shadows, made his way to the parking lot behind the cafe and recording studio. He ducked under the police line and picked his way as quietly as possible through the debris and broken glass which covered the pavement. In two graceful leaps he was up the concrete steps and into the darkness of the cafe's back doorway. The door was locked but the doorjamb, splintered earlier by the police, had not been tacked back together. With just a little pressure he was inside. It was easy, perhaps a little too easy.

Rurrik quickly pulled the door closed behind him and squatted down in the cover of an upturned table. The acrid smell of charred wood stung the inside of his nostrils. He listened. Only the occasional drip of water from the ceiling to the floor could be heard. The young Russian slowly raised his head above the table. He surveyed the interior of the cafe in the dim light. It was a depressing sight. Beer bottles, dishes of food, and shards of glass covered the floor along with broken tables, chairs, ceiling tiles, and puddles of water. His inner sense told him that Taylor's was empty, and he was alone. The FBI agents were not here yet. Still, he was glad Margaret had stayed in the car. The sight of the cafe would have made her cry.

He made his way quickly to the Multimixer, lifted the top, and fumbled around inside, eventually retrieving the canister. Just as quickly he retreated from the cafe, across the parking lot, and back under the police line.

The darkness was nearly complete as he came in sight of the old DeSoto on Monroe Street. The car was as he left it, but something seemed wrong. Margaret was not in the passenger's seat; in fact, he could not see her at all. "She must be lying down to get some rest," he reasoned as he removed the metal tape canister from his oversized jacket pocket.

Rurrik approached the car gingerly so as not to startle the sleeping girl and bent over to see inside. She was neither in the front seat nor in the back. Rurrik straightened with a start and as he did Van Pelt took hold of his arms and pulled them behind his back. The pain caused him to drop the metal tape canister.

"I've got your ass now, you commie bastard," Van Pelt said as he pushed the slender Russian against the old car hard enough to cause rust to fall from the quarter panels.

"Take it easy, Van Pelt. We don't need to attract unnecessary attention," Peal cautioned. "It's the tape we're after. Let's just get it and then we can go home."

"The damn thing rolled under the car," Van Pelt said.

"I'll hold the boy; you get the tape."

Van Pelt let go of Rurrik's arm and knelt down to peer under the car. The young Russian twisted free of Peal's grip and spun toward freedom. Van Pelt, still in the kneeling position, shot out his foot and caught Rurrik's instep. The Russian fell to the sidewalk with Van Pelt quickly on top of him.

"Try to hold on to him if you can," Van Pelt advised as he handed Rurrik back over to Peal and retrieved the metal canister. He stood up and put it in the pocket of his coat. "Let's kill this communist. It would be the patriotic thing to do."

"If we kill him, we have to kill her too and, although she may not look like one, she is an American citizen," Peal cautioned.

"What the hell, throw him in the trunk with his coolie girlfriend. They can keep each other warm until morning."

The two agents hustled Rurrik around to the back of the car and sprung the trunk lid. Inside Margaret was huddled on the discarded merchant marine greatcoat. "I'm sorry Rurrik. These two goons told me if I tried to warn you, they would kill us both."

"She called us goons," Van Pelt shoved Rurrik down into the trunk and pulled his gun. "Let's plug them both."

Peal pushed Van Pelt's gun hand down. "We got the tape. It's over."

Van Pelt pulled the tape canister from his pocket and tossed it into the air. Catching it deftly, he poked it toward the young Russian's face.

"Watch your fingers," Peal said as he pushed the trunk lid closed.

"I called you goons because you are goons... Hey! You can't leave us in here, we'll suffocate. You're not goons, you're worse than..." Margaret's speech was cut off as Rurrik clamped his hand over her mouth.

Rurrik's eyes adjusted quickly to the darkness. Shafts of dim light filtered in through the bullet holes in the trunk lid and rusted fabric of the fender wells. "Wait until they are gone and then we need to find something to pop the trunk lid from the inside," Rurrik took his hand from her mouth. "There are tools in here someplace. A screwdriver or pliers would work." He could feel the warmth of Margaret's breath and smell its sweetness as the two shifted to find more room.

"How about this?" Margaret asked as she freed Muscadine's pistol from the pocket of the greatcoat and held it close to the Russian's face.

"We cannot use that in here," Rurrik redirected the gun.

"But we can shoot them if they are still there when we get out can't we?"

Rurrik found the tire iron and managed to pop the trunk lid. Margaret vaulted over him and landed on the pavement like a cat. She spun around pointing the gun as if it were a compass needle seeking true north. Rurrik tumbled to the street and, ducking under the gun, grabbed Margaret by the wrist. "We must go."

"They know better than to come back here."

"They will come back. They will come back for the tape, and we must be gone."

"But they have the tape, don't they?"

Rurrik pulled the roll of audio tape from the game pouch on the back of his jacket. "I'm afraid they have drive wheel for Multimixer. It will not make them happy. We must go and go quickly."

Rurrik slid behind the wheel of the old car and Margaret got in on the passenger's side. "They took the keys," she said.

"Is not problem," Rurrik said as he reached under the dash and jumped the ignition wires.

"Will it be safe to go to the hospital to check on Sam and Gizmo?" Margaret asked.

"I don't know. Maybe if we go quickly."

The nurse behind the desk flipped the papers on her clipboard and looked out over her glasses at Margaret and Rurrik. "Excuse me, we are here to see Sam Philips and Gizmo Broussard," Margaret said.

"Seven twelve," the nurse said as she looked back down at her clipboard.

"They are in room seven twelve?" Margaret asked.

The nurse placed her clipboard on the counter and, looking up at the two, pointed with her thumb at the clock on the wall behind her. "Twelve past seven. Visiting hours ended at seven."

"Can you tell us anything of their condition?" Margaret asked.

The nurse looked from Margaret to Rurrik and then back again. "Not unless you are next-of-kin which I sincerely doubt. Besides, I believe those two are no longer with us."

"No longer with us?" Rurrik repeated.

"Gone," the nurse said as she picked up the clipboard and turned to leave. "And, if you ask me, we are all better for it… Musicians." The nurse passed through a door behind the counter and closed it after her.

"What does she mean - gone?" Rurrik asked as he and Margaret stood alone in the reception area.

"I'm not sure."

An Asian orderly approached them from a side corridor. "Please, come with me," he said in a low voice.

Margaret and Rurrik followed him down the corridor, through a door, and into a stairwell. "Nurse Chaney is not a tolerant person," the orderly said as he shut the stairwell door behind them.

"She lacks a certain charm," Margaret said to the orderly. "Do I know you?"

"You are Margaret Soo. I am Harold Choi. I used to go with my father to deliver vegetables to your parents in Marigold."

"Harold! I'm sorry I didn't recognize you." Margaret gave the orderly a hug.

"I would not have known you if I had not seen your picture with Elvis," Harold explained. "Your friend Gizmo is still here. We may be able to catch him if we hurry."

As they started down the stairway Harold spoke back over his shoulder. "Mr. Phillips was treated and released. Mr. Broussard's injuries were of a more serious nature; concussion, some broken ribs. He needed quite a few stitches."

"Will he be alright?" Rurrik asked.

"He is being released," Harold said. "Mr. Broussard is a determined man. His wife Maureen is here, and I even heard that Mr. Fats Domino is sending an ambulance to transport him back to New Orleans."

Harold led them down a wide corridor and pushed open a door that led out onto a loading dock behind the hospital. The dimly lit parking lot stretched out to a brick border wall that

208

separated it from the street. Harold scanned the parking area and looked out toward the gap in the wall that formed the hospital's main entrance. "I do not see the ambulance, perhaps it is not here yet."

As they watched, a long black vehicle rolled through the hospital entrance and began to make its way through the parking lot. "Could that be it?" Rurrik asked.

"That's not an ambulance, it's a hearse," Margaret said.

"I don't understand," Harold said. "We have no pickups scheduled for this evening."

"Do FBI agents drive hearse?" Rurrik asked.

Margaret and Rurrik grabbed Harold and pulled him along with them back through the door and off the loading dock. The hearse approached slowly and then backed into one of the marked slots in front of the dock. There was a long pause and then the driver's side door opened and Muscadine Bolivar stepped out.

Margaret burst out through the door and leaped from the loading dock. She threw her arms around the big man's neck. "Muscadine, am I ever glad to see you. This whole thing is like a bad dream. They shot at us and chased us through the snow and then locked us in the trunk."

"It's gonna be alright now," Muscadine said. "Fats felt real bad about what happened. He's convinced that the bombers were after him and got Sam and Gizmo by mistake... By the way Margaret, I was so sorry to hear about Buddy. I know you two were close."

Margaret pushed away from the big man and looked up into his face. "What happened to Buddy?"

Muscadine put his hands on her shoulders. "You didn't hear? His plane went down in Iowa. Killed them all; Buddy, Ritchie, Jape, and the pilot. Maybe Waylon too. I'm so sorry."

Margaret put her hand down to steady herself and sat on the edge of the loading dock. "We got there too late. The plane was already in the air."

"The agents chased us. They shot the car," Rurrik said as he and Harold came out onto the loading dock. "Joey Cicero was with them. He is spy."

"Cicero. I'll have to have a talk with that boy," Muscadine said.

The automatic double doors at the opposite end of the loading dock levered open and Maureen emerged pushing Gizmo in a wheelchair. Gizmo was swinging a cane around and talking back over his shoulder. "You stop this thing right now. I'm not riding to New Orleans in the back of an ambulance, those things ride like trucks. Only fit for folks who are unconscious, delirious, or dead."

"You'll do what you're told, or I'll turn Muscadine loose on you," Maureen said.

Gizmo looked around for the first time. "Muscadine, I didn't even see you there. And look, there's Rurrik and Peggy Soo. And I see you've met Harold, he's just about the only one in this hospital with any sense. The only one missing is Prince Albert."

"The Prince is staying with the Domino family," Muscadine said. "He loves it there on Caffin Avenue and they love him. That whole bunch is playing music all the time. Of course, Rose Marie is insisting The Prince start going to school with the rest of the gang."

"She plans to make a productive citizen out of him, does she?" Gizmo noticed the hearse for the first time. "Oh no, that ain't an ambulance it's a corpse coach. They ride even worse. They're a major factor in the increasing popularity of cremation."

"We couldn't get an ambulance on such short notice," Muscadine apologized.

"What's the matter with Margaret?" Gizmo asked

Muscadine looked over at the girl who sat alone on the edge of the loading dock. "She just found out about Buddy,"

Maureen went over and sat beside Margaret. "I heard about it yesterday on my way up here. Everybody on the bus was talking. Those poor young boys."

"If only we had gotten there sooner..." Margaret said. "They shot at us. They shot your car Gizmo."

"If you got there any sooner, they would have killed you as well," Muscadine said.

"They will shoot us all when they find out this," Rurrik pulled the tape from his coat. "They will not quit."

"Is that the Super Session? Well praise be, I thought all that was lost for good," Gizmo laughed "Sam is going to be delighted. That man was more upset about losing the music than he was about losing his entire recording studio."

"I have heard about the Super Session. Is that actually a copy of it?" Harold asked.

Gizmo pointed with his cane at the reel of recording tape. "Far as I know it's the only copy. We gotta take care of it."

Harold walked over to a large cardboard box by the trash cans. He reached in and took out a metal film canister, opened it up, and dumped out the film. "The hospital has just upgraded its training films to 8mm. This stuff is going to the dump," he said as he handed the empty canister to Rurrik.

"That will protect the tape but what's going to protect Rurrik? They're bound to figure him to come here to the hospital. Might be on their way now. We gotta act and act quickly," Gizmo said as he waved his cane like a general with a swagger stick. "Is my car here or were its wounds critical?"

"This is no time to start fussing about your car," Maureen said.

Gizmo spun his chair to face the group. "You listen up now. Rurrik, go get my car and be quick about it. Maureen, you and I are going on a motor trip through the birthplace of the Blues while Muscadine drives these two back to New Orleans in the hearse."

Rurrik, in response to Gizmo's order, was gone in a flash but Maureen balked. "But I don't understand."

"They'll be looking for two young people in my old DeSoto and when they find the car, they'll find disappointment... You'll love it sugar pie. It will be like the honeymoon we never had," Gizmo said.

"How sweet. It will go nicely with the wedding we never had." Maureen said as she rolled her eyes.

Rurrik returned with the DeSoto and backed it into the slot beside the larger black vehicle. As he got out of the car, he stood on the running board and looked out toward the gate to the street. A dark sedan was pulling into the hospital grounds. "They are coming!"

"Let's just lay low and take it easy. They can't see the DeSoto, it's blocked by the coffin caddie," Gizmo said. "Every G-man I ever met has been an arrogant SOB. I'll bet anything they will pull around front and park in the emergency lane outside the main entrance. They will be going in the front door. We will be heading out the back." The group took cover as the sedan passed the entrance to the parking lot.

Rurrik eased his way to the front of the hearse and peeked out over the hood. The dark sedan stopped and then backed up. Rurrik flattened on the pavement. The sedan paused and then drove on and passed from view.

Muscadine and Maureen loaded Gizmo into the old DeSoto as quickly as possible in view of his injuries. Maureen noticed the back seat was full of gas station give-aways. "And there are all our wedding gifts, how thoughtful."

"Fats has the apartment above his garage ready for Gizmo," Muscadine said.

"That's very kind of Mr. Domino but Gizmo will be staying with me," Maureen said as she got behind the wheel.

Harold the orderly slid the box of obsolete training films across the loading dock toward the back of the DeSoto. "Take these with you."

"We don't have time to take out the trash," Muscadine said.

"Harold may be onto something here," Gizmo said. "Muscadine, if you don't mind could you just put that box into the trunk." Muscadine lifted the heavy box with ease and dropped it into the trunk of the DeSoto.

Margaret got into the back of the hearse and Muscadine climbed in behind the wheel. Rurrik stood on the back bumper of the hearse and waved his arm in a forward motion. "We take them to Missouri."

"Missouri?" Margaret said.

"Mr. John Wayne said that in movie Red River," Rurrik said as the hearse lurched forward. Margaret yanked him down into the back of the vehicle and pulled the doors closed behind him. The hearse pulled out with the DeSoto right behind it. The small convoy passed through the gates in the brick wall and disappeared into the night just as Peal and Van Pelt came out onto the loading dock. All the two agents found was Harold cleaning up around the garbage cans.

Van Pelt took the orderly by the shoulder, spun him around, and brought him face to face with the agent's FBI badge. "Has anybody been out here?" Harold cow-towed and spoke in Mandarin. Van Pelt pushed the orderly hard into the trash cans. "Another damn Chinaman. This one doesn't even speak English."

CHAPTER 17

The interior of the hearse had been converted to transport the living with a cot down one side topped with a mattress, blankets, and pillows. But the black window curtains and somber decor of the interior spoke of the dead. A wall-mounted vase held lilies. Two folding chairs sat on the side away from the cot. Margaret and Rurrik tried the chairs and found them to be quite comfortable. The hearse made its way to Highway 61 south, left Memphis behind, and headed out into the Delta. In no time the two weary travelers were both asleep.

There was a small window between the front and back of the hearse. Rurrik and Margaret woke with a start as Muscadine slid it open. "Take a look out to starboard."

Rurrik moved to the window on the left side of the hearse. Margaret took hold of his arm and directed him to the right-hand window. A steady rain was falling, and traffic was moving slowly. A dark sedan and Gizmo's DeSoto were pulled over on the shoulder. Peal and Van Pelt stood beside the rear of the DeSoto. Peal was holding a flashlight while Van Pelt opened one of the metal film canisters from the box in the trunk. He inspected the contents of the canister and then threw it into a pile that spread around his feet. The canister bounced off the pile and rolled out into the highway. Muscadine swerved to avoid the canister and splashed water over the two agents.

"That should hold them a while," Muscadine said. "Do you want me to take you over to Fats' place when we get back?"

"I'm afraid we would be putting Fats and his family in danger. Those films will slow them up, but they won't stop," Margaret said.

Rurrik sat down on the cot. "I will go back to my ship,"

Margaret sat on the cot as well and looked at Rurrik in disbelief. "Back to your ship? Back to Russia?"

"It is best choice. In Russia they will be pleased to make copies of the tape. They will distribute throughout America to corrupt the youth. The music will be saved."

"What about you?" Margaret said. "Will you be safe there?"

"I do not know what happen to me. Perhaps I will be rewarded for doing job so well. Perhaps not. FBI will not follow me to Russia. You tell them tape is gone, they will not harm you," Rurrik said.

Margaret put her hand on Rurrik's arm. "You can't go back to Russia. It's cold and dark there and the food is bad."

"I would sure hate to see ole' Rurrik leave, he is a true hero of Rock & Roll," Muscadine said. "But he may be right. Those G-men ain't foolin'."

Tears came up in Margaret's eyes. "But you just can't go."

"It is best choice," Rurrik put his arm around Margaret. She leaned her head against his shoulder, and he kissed her forehead.

"If you get tired, I drive," Rurrik said to Muscadine.

"Don't you worry about me. I'm good all night long. I don't view sleep as a necessity, more like a luxury item." Muscadine slid the window shut.

The eastern sky was still dark as the long black car sailed around the gentle arch of the Lake Pontchartrain causeway and into the city of New Orleans. The hearse glided to a perfect stop in front of a warehouse on Poydras Street. The Canal Street entrance to the wharf, the spot where Rurrik's American odyssey had begun, was just a block to the west but hidden from view by the warehouse. The driver's door opened and Rurrik stepped out while Margaret exited from the passenger's side. The two walked around to the back of the vehicle and Rurrik tapped gently on the doors.

"That will never do," Margaret slapped the flat of her hand against the door panel.

A wino, sleeping in the doorway to the warehouse was awakened and sat up. "Bang all you want. Won't do no good. You can't wake the dead. I know, I've tried."

The back doors of the hearse opened and Muscadine stepped out into the cool night air. "Ain't it good to be alive?" He handed a lily to Margaret. The wino pulled his coat over his head and turned his back to the group.

Margaret, Rurrik, and Muscadine walked to the end of the block and found a place where they could stand in the shadow of the warehouse and see the main entrance to the wharf. Even in the pre-dawn hours, there was activity as people came and went. Rurrik noticed a group of eight or nine men in work clothes jockeying for position around a fire barrel. There were several other smaller gatherings in doorways and around the trucks that lined the curb. The entrance was well lit, but collars and hats shadowed most of the faces.

"I don't see those agents," Margaret said.

"Perhaps we are here faster than they are here," Rurrik said "But they could have called other FBI. Any men could be agents."

"Why don't we just go in the back door?" Muscadine nodded his head to the west. Two blocks down, a single streetlight illuminated a small guard house that watched over a side gate to the docks. An old black man sat in the guard's station reading a newspaper.

"What berth is your ship tied up at?" Muscadine asked Rurrik as they approached the booth. Rurrik could not remember.

"Well, how about the name of your ship?"

"Sabboto Noch," Rurrik replied.

Muscadine approached the guard. "May I help you?" the old man asked.

"Why yes," Muscadine replied. "We would like to know what berth the Samantha Something-or-other is tied up at."

"Excuse me, sir?" the old black man said.

Margaret stepped up to the window. "We are looking for the Sabboto Noch, a Soviet freighter. Could you tell us what berth she is tied up at?"

"I'm not supposed to give that information out to just anybody," the old man said. "But I couldn't give you that number even if I wanted to. She sailed."

Margaret smiled but Rurrik stepped forward. "Are you sure?"

"Say man, don't you have to look at a chart or something like that?" Muscadine asked.

"Don't have to. Got it all right here," the old man tapped his finger above one eye. "Oh my, you're Muscadine Bolivar? Well I'll be. I saw you fight more than once. You were the best."

A broad smile crossed Muscadine's face. "Ezzard Charles would give you an argument on that. Say, my friend here needs to leave town as soon as possible. I wonder if you could help us out." Muscadine took out a crisp bill, folded it lengthwise, and extended it through the window of the guardhouse.

"In a hurry to go, are you?" the old guard looked at Rurrik as he took the bill from Muscadine.

Muscadine leaned over toward the window. "Let's just say that my friend needs to book passage tonight."

"And where would your friend like to book passage to?" the guard asked.

"At this point, he is more concerned with the 'from' part than the 'to' part. Just about any ship will do, just so's going 'from' here. But no banana boats," Muscadine said.

"Well, let's see… The *Zod* is in berth 17. They should be the next ship out. Turkish registry but the crew is mostly Armenian," the old black man said. Muscadine and the guard looked at Rurrik. The young Russian shook his head.

The guard leaned forward and lowered his voice. "The *Conroy* is after the *Zod* but she's an American ship and I take it you are not interested in the domestic market."

"Definitely not," Muscadine said.

The guard straightened back up. "How about the *Timaru*. New Zealand registry. Not a sober lot but good folks. The purser is a Maori."

"A what?" Muscadine asked.

"New Zealand aboriginal. A man of color," the old guard explained.

"They got colored people in New Zealand?" Muscadine asked.

"As black as you and me… berth 17," the guard pointed down the wharf toward the west and away from the main gate.

Rurrik was glad to be going that way. The light was dimmer in that direction and the ships tended to be more shopworn. As they approached the gangplank to the *Timaru,* Muscadine steered Rurrik and Margaret to a shadowy alcove between piles of freight. "You two wait here while I go on board and speak to this fellow man of color."

"I want to go with you," Margaret blurted out.

"It might be better if I handle..." Muscadine began to answer but stopped when he saw that Margaret was talking to Rurrik and not to him.

"You want to go to New Zealand?" Rurrik asked.

"To New Zealand or wherever. I want to go with you, Rurrik."

"But your job, your family..." Rurrik said. "You will not know people in New Zealand."

"Taylor's was my job, and the studio was my family. They're all gone now. I don't want to go back to Memphis. I'll know one person in New Zealand, I'll know you. I want to go with you Rurrik, if you want me to."

"Yes, I want you to. I want you to very much," Rurrik said.

"Passage for two." Muscadine left the two young lovers in an embrace.

Margaret and Rurrik sat on a crate to await Muscadine's return.

"Do you know anything about New Zealand?" Margaret asked.

"I do not."

"I guess you never got there during your hitch in the Soviet Merchant Marines."

Rurrik laughed. "If they have people of color in New Zealand, do you think they might have red beans and rice?

"I don't know but we will find out together," Margaret kissed him.

"Well, isn't this charming," Van Pelt said.

Rurrik and Margaret broke their embrace to face agent Van Pelt who stood at the entrance to the alcove with his gun in one hand and an empty metal canister in the other. Agent Peal stood by his side.

"Hey, Van Pelt, seen any good movies lately?" Margaret asked.

Van Pelt raised his gun. "I should have killed you both back in Memphis. Say sayonara."

Peal grabbed Van Pelt's gun hand. "They're just kids."

Van Pelt pushed Peal aside and then pointed the gun at his fellow agent. "Stay out of my way Peal. I'm telling you for the last time, this God damned Rock & Roll has got to be stopped,"

Peal held his hands up to try and calm Van Pelt. "Easy now, you're taking this thing far too seriously. You and Hoover both.

This music is just a fad. It will run its course in a year or so if we all just stand down and let it. Don't take it personal."

Van Pelt lowered his gun. "It is personal, it's personal to me." Tears of anger began to form in his eyes. "My wife left me. She ran off with a drummer."

"Your wife left you for a salesman?" Peal asked.

"Not a salesman, you fool, a damned drummer in a band," Tears ran down Van Pelt's cheeks. "My wife would rather live in sin with a Rock & Roll drummer than to live with me."

Margaret stepped in front of Rurrik. "I'd rather live in dirt with weasels. I'd rather put on a tin bill and go peck in the yard with the chickens. I'd rather..."

Van Pelt spun back toward the girl and raised his gun.

Peal lunged for Van Pelt's arm. "It's only Rock & Roll,"

Van Pelt pushed the older agent aside and then struck him across the temple with the gun. Peal fell to the ground motionless as Rurrik leaped toward Van Pelt. The agent raised his gun and fired, the bullet striking Rurrik's head. The young Russian spun around and fell to the ground at Margaret's feet.

"Stop right there," Margaret drew Muscadine's gun and leveled it at Van Pelt.

A smile twisted the agent's lip. "Here's a surprise. What you gonna do China doll? Gonna shoot me?"

"I will if I have to. Put the gun down."

The agent slowly placed his gun on top of a fifty-five-gallon drum by his side. Rurrik groaned. Blood oozed from an ugly crease just below his hair line.

"If you're gonna shoot me you better do it quickly and tend to your boyfriend. He's leaking pretty bad. A man can bleed out, same as a hog."

Margaret looked down at Rurrik and then back at Van Pelt who was advancing toward her. She tried to pull the trigger and then, breaking into tears, threw the gun at the agent and dropped to Rurrik's side. Van Pelt retrieved his pistol and leveled it at Margaret's head.

She looked up to face her executioner. Her expression, a mixture of fear and anger, turned to one of amusement. Van Pelt froze and then began to turn.

BLANG! Muscadine brought an empty fifty-five gallon barrel down over the agent's head and body. Van Pelt, still encased in the barrel, slumped to the ground.

Margaret ran to the big man and threw her arms around him. "He shot Rurrik."

Muscadine dropped to one knee beside the Russian who was beginning to regain consciousness. The ex-fighter inspected the wound, removed his silk scarf, and quickly fashioned a bandage. "I've seen worse. A good cut man would have him right back in the ring. Let's get on the ship before these two wakes up and I have to KO them all over again."

On board the Timaru a narrow passageway led to a cramped but clean cabin. "Cozy," Margaret observed.

"Extremely cozy," Muscadine said. "But everything's been arranged. You two should stay out of sight until the ship reaches international waters. They will bring you food and whatever else you need."

"Will you be all right?" Margaret asked.

"Didn't neither of them agents see me. If I get out of here before they come round, I'll be fine," Muscadine handed a small wad of bills to Margaret. "Not much left here, these romantic cruises ain't cheap, but it should get you by for a few days when you make port."

"How can we repay you?" Rurrik asked.

"You just make copies of that Super Session," Muscadine said as a warning bell sounded and the pitch of the ship's engines stepped up a notch. "You still got the tape, don't you?"

Rurrik patted the canister in his jacket pocket. "I will find somebody for make copies for whole world. I will do as soon as we get to New Zealand,"

"Oh, well, about that, I should tell you that this here ship ain't going directly to New Zealand. They got a few stops to make first," Muscadine said as he turned to leave. "And by the way, I didn't have enough cash on hand to send you all the way to New Zealand. You'll be getting off at the first stop."

"Where is the first stop?" Margaret asked.

A second bell rang, and the sound of the engines intensified. Muscadine turned back over his shoulder as he hurried down the corridor toward the exit. "You know, I'm not certain but it's somewhere overseas. For a fellow man of color that Aborigine sure talked funny. You take care of Rurrik's head and lay low for a day or two."

"No problem," Margaret put her arms around Rurrik and pulled him into the cabin.

The Timaru was far into the Gulf of Mexico when Margaret and Rurrik ventured out of the cabin and onto the deck. It was a clear morning with the sea breeze coming from the south. The two stood at the railing and looked out over the cerulean waters.

Margaret pulled her jacket tight against the steady ocean breeze. "It's so beautiful. I can easily see how a mariner such as yourself could fall in love with the sea,"

Rurrik stood behind Margaret and wrapped his arms around her. A deckhand walked past them.

"Where does the ship go now?" Rurrik asked.

"U.K." was the deckhand's curt reply.

"U.K.?" Margaret asked.

"Yes, mum," the deckhand said. "United Kingdom, we're bound for Liverpool."

The deck hand went about his business and the two young voyagers looked back out over the sea.

"I don't know anything about Liverpool but, from everything I've heard, the people in England are very white. I doubt they will have red beans and rice," Margaret said.

"I wonder if they will have Rock & Roll."

The End